Fighting for Infinity

ALYSON ROOT

J&M Books

For permission requests, write to a.rootauthor@alysonroot.com

Published by J&M Books

Lytchett House, 13 Freeland Park, Wareham Road, Poole, Dorset, BH16 6FA

Print ISBN: 978-1-917785-09-9

Ebook ISBN: 978-1-917785-27-3

Developmental Edit & Cover design by:

Tara Sullivan, The Write Gal Co.

www.thewritegal.com

Proofread by:

Crystal Lee Wren, COLProof

Infinity is forever, and that is what you are to me, you are
my forever
— Sandi Lynn

One

AMELIA

My dreams are a continuous loop of the night in our honeymoon suite. Two weeks have passed and still, the dreams come. I can smell the body odor of the soldiers as if they were standing right next to me. I shouldn't have let them live. It's my one regret.

"You're no killer, my love." Erin's voice is quiet in the darkness. I pull her closer to my body.

"I wasn't. But things have changed, Erin. We won't come out of this without bloodshed. It's inevitable." My worst nightmare has come true. Humans have lived up to my expectations. I'd so desperately hoped that I'd be proven wrong, but they did exactly what history told us they would do. They chose violence over peace. Hatred instead of understanding.

My people and my family are scattered in the wind, too scared to stay in their homes. Erin and Mohan are the only ones in communication. Erin assures me our family is safe. Mohan was able to get the word out long before the government attacked. Reaching us was harder due to our...let's say, other activities. Our minds were only connected to each other.

"Amelia, we don't know how this will play out."

Sitting up, I scrub my face. Erin's optimism is grating on me. "Erin, we've been on the run for two weeks. We are literally being hunted by the military. *That* is how it's playing out. Do you think I won't fight back if they find us?"

"Please come back here," she says, pulling on my arm. How I wish our problems could be resolved by being in one another's arms. Reluctantly, I slide back down, and she curls into my side. "We cross the border tomorrow. You will feel better when you see the family."

It has taken us this long to reach the American border. Escaping Hawaii with as much luggage as we could carry from our holiday was no easy venture. But my name and now Erin's hold water amongst our kind. We were never short of vampires willing to help us return home. That is the thing the president did not account for. She attacked prematurely, showing her hand. If she were a smart woman, she'd have gathered more information first. Then she would have known how many vampires she was declaring war on. The imbecile will piss her pants when it comes to light.

"I'll feel better when I no longer have to worry about agents trying to kill us."

"They couldn't if they tried," Erin mutters into my shoulder. Yes, another thing I'm sure the president is unaware of. Sending soldiers with guns to kill us was and is a fruitless order. Neither Erin nor I will die from bullet wounds. It will piss me off though, and if that happens, I'm not entirely sure I'll be able to restrain the other side of me. The new, raging side of my personality that is growing stronger every day.

"Yes, you can," Erin says, her head lifting to look into my eyes. The advantage and sometimes disadvantage of my wife reading my thoughts. "That side of you is strong, but it is there to help, not hurt."

"It's there to protect too, Erin. I will protect you and my people with every cell of my being. You need to know that."

Ever since our change, we are learning new things about ourselves. Erin is mastering her ability to enter people's minds. To see their memories and exist in their present. I am learning to hone my heightened senses. I can see for miles with crystal-clear vision now. My hearing is so acute I can hear the sweat drop off a person's body, from hundreds of feet away. As for my speed, well, I've never been one for exercise, but lately my body craves running. The world blurs as I move. I doubt there is a single human or vampire on this planet that could outrun me.

"I do know that. And I know things aren't good. I'm not being obtuse, but if we only think of the worst-case scenario, we won't get through this, Amelia. Can we concentrate on getting to the family, and then figure out the rest?"

Sometimes I forget that Erin probably feels this more keenly than I. She was a human only a few months ago. It was she who convinced me not to tar all humans with the same brush. Such a shame the second they have a chance to prove themselves to be more than savages, they fail so miserably.

Sleep, my love.

I heed Erin's advice and settle deeper into her embrace. Tomorrow, we will cross from Mexico to the

US, and then we are but a few hours from reuniting with our family. Mohan has worked tirelessly to get everything set up. From what Erin has told me, there is quite an underground community of vampires now. It all feels so Hollywood. So many times, I scoffed at the movies that depicted this kind of scenario. Yet here we are. Although, if we end up holed up in anything resembling an abandoned church, I am going to lose it.

Erin chuckles, her body gently vibrating against me. At least she finds my pondering amusing. "You are dramatic at times, Amelia. Now, please, sleep."

I huff playfully, then kiss her temple. "Fine. Goodnight, my love."

My dream replays as usual. When I awake, Erin is caressing my face gently with the tips of her fingers. It's how she soothes me, and I'm so very grateful. We spend a few moments simply looking at each other. Our world may be in turmoil, but that doesn't mean I will ever lose focus on the most important thing. Erin. My love for her and our bond. Just a few moments of gazing into her eyes reminds me of our power. I'm not referring to our new abilities, but the one that existed from the second I laid eyes on Erin. The power of our souls finding each other. Together, we can do anything. I truly believe that.

"We should get going soon, honey," she whispers.

"Just a few more minutes," I plead. She nods and leans down to kiss me. Erin is adept at entering my mind now. She has mastered the art of projecting her feelings onto me. Right now, she is sending me calm and patience. I'd be insulted if her intentions weren't spot on. I am impatient to get home, and every time I think of what has happened to us, I am less than calm.

We rise and dress. Rosa is waiting in the kitchen for us. She is just one of many vampires who have put their safety on the line to help us. Our celebrity has spread farther than either Erin or I could comprehend. For once, I am grateful for it. Without help, I dread to think where we would be.

"Good morning," Rosa says with a bow of her head. That is also something that is now the norm for us both. Being treated like vampire royalty, whether we agree or not with the sentiment. Erin protested in the beginning, but eventually gave up. Especially when she saw what it meant to those who had chosen to help us.

"Good morning, Rosa." Erin embraces her, and I smile at Rosa's red-tinged cheeks. "Did you sleep well?"

"Perfectly. Shall we eat?"

The soft morning light dances in the air. The cicadas are still chirping as we settle at the table outside, with a carafe of Red and a veritable feast of Mexican food. At times, I wish we could just stay here, surrounded by the beauty and peace of Rosa's land. It would be so much easier. And then I am reminded why we cannot. My body reacts before anyone else is aware there are vampires approaching. I can sense the agitation of the human with them. She is desperate.

"We have company," I say, putting my glass of Red on the table and standing. Moments later, a car winds its way to Rosa's house. Three vampires and a human exit the vehicle. One by one, they approach the table, stopping a few feet away before bowing their heads. I stuff down the urge to roll my eyes.

"My queens," the oldest begins. I hold up my hand, but it's Erin who speaks.

"Less of that, please." She smiles. "I'm Erin, and this is Amelia. You need help." It's not a question. We both know the youngest vampire and the human are together, and in need of our talents.

"Erin," the vampire begins. "My name is Horatio, and this is my husband, Emilio. Our son, Ricco, and his mate, Paula."

"Very nice to meet you," I say, stepping forward to shake their hands.

"We've traveled for days, hoping to find you," Emilio chokes. He is full of emotion. "I didn't think we would, but Horatio told us to have faith, and he was right."

Erin steps to my side. "You will turn thirty this evening," she says, addressing Ricco.

"Yes," he replies quietly.

"And you have mated?" I ask, looking Paula in the eye. They nod. I know Horatio already introduced Paula as Ricco's mate, but I have to hear it from them. It's almost a stipulation of this new side of me. I can only help the human if I have eye contact and confirmation of their need. Like Erin, I form a tentative bond with each one I turn.

We are in a bind. Time is of the essence to get back to our family, but neither Erin nor I can turn away from vampires and humans who need our help.

"You will need to travel with us," I begin. "Erin and I must cross the border today."

"We will go with you, and do anything you need," Horatio states. "It would be our honor."

"Then let us prepare." Erin adds, "Have you eaten?"

The family shakes their head. Rosa is already fetching more glasses and plates. Erin does what she does best and puts everyone at ease. I find it harder when I have a human close to me that needs to be changed. Even though

Ricco has not yet turned 30—when vampires undergo their cellular transformation to become fully immortal—I can already sense the strength of their bond. I can *feel* Paula's human soul yearning to be bonded for eternity with her mate. It tugs on my heart and causes my anxiety to spike. The feeling will not abate until Paula is a vampire. It's going to be a long day.

Rosa sends us off with enough food and Red to feed a small village. Erin has assured me she was able to contact Mohan and update him on our current situation and the new members of our party. Hopefully, Mohan can get in touch with the vampire who is tasked with sneaking us across the border in the next three hours.

The new additions put us at a disadvantage in that I cannot pick them all up and run full speed through the desert to the meeting place. That was the original plan. Erin is as light as a feather and would have easily settled into my body as I ran. Now, we have to walk.

"Honey, please stop grumbling," Erin says softly as we trek. "We will only be a few hours behind schedule and Mohan isn't worried."

"I apologize," I reply. She's right, of course. It is far more important that we help Ricco and Paula. My impatience stems from a mix of fatigue and frustration.

I know we have a responsibility to help our brothers and sisters, but now and then a frisson of fear grips me when I think of Erin in harm's way because of the so-called "prophecy" we are burdened with. Maybe I'd feel better if I had a say in it, but that's not the case. It's a go-along-with-the-flow kind of scenario. I'm not great with those.

The day slips by as we walk. The family is quiet, which is understandable. I'm sure Horatio and Emilio have been sick with worry, believing their son would fall into madness if they didn't find us.

"There," Erin says, pointing. I've been lost in my thoughts and didn't notice the border fence.

My eyes focus on a distant figure. He's wearing a Border Patrol uniform and is leaning against his SUV, looking in our direction. "That's him," I say. "Let's go." I pick up the pace, and everyone follows without a word. We reach the fence and the vampire waiting for us in around ten minutes. He smiles and bows. This time, I do roll my eyes. I'm *so* done with today. I want to get the hell out of here, and to our safe house where I can wash up, rest, and then prepare for Ricco's change at midnight.

"I'm glad to see you. My name is Jeremy. Mohan sends his love. I'm going to take you straight to the safe house."

"Thank you, Jeremy," Erin replies. She gestures to the fence. "Shall we?"

One by one, the family climbs up and over. Once they are safely on the other side, Erin and I hold hands and jump, clearing the fence easily. We land effortlessly. All eyes are on us as we straighten our clothes. I still forget most vampires and humans have yet to witness anything like us in real life.

"Off we go then," Erin says, smiling. The family and Jeremy seem to jolt out of their shock and awe-like state.

There will definitely be more bowing now. Ugh.

Two

ERIN

Hold it together for a little while longer, Erin.

The phrase has been my mantra for the past two weeks. I'd like nothing more than to break down into a mess of fear and anxiety, but what good would that do? It certainly wouldn't help Amelia. I can feel her battling her new self on a daily basis.

She is scared to let her new abilities fully form. I think the incident with Mack scared her. That feeling of being out of control. Even though she has turned dozens and dozens of humans by now, her first experience left a scar. There is anger within her, but it isn't spiteful. It is a protective righteousness. Her inner warrior and protector is itching to be unleashed but, my love is scared to lose control of it. I read her so easily. In her dreams I wander through her mind, trying to plant seeds of confidence. Amelia Loch is the strongest woman I know, and there is no doubt in my heart that if she allowed herself to be the vampire she is clearly destined to be, she would flourish.

Amelia's reticence comes from a place of learned fear. As much as she scoffs at humans and their idiotic mythology concerning vampires, I can see it is those very myths she is terrified of. I understand. I mean, she has become stronger, faster and has fangs, unlike other vampires. All traits that humans have written about over history. So, in her mind, it's feasible to believe she could inherit other characteristics, such as blood-lust and violence. That's where I disagree. Amelia is not a monster. She is my other half. There is only light in her heart, no shadow or darkness. But will she listen? Of course not, because she is friggin' stubborn as a mule!

So, until I can get her to accept herself entirely, I need to be the strong one. Thankfully, I've had Mohan available for chats. As crazy as the past two weeks have been, just hearing general day-to-day updates from the Grand Master has been just the thing I needed. Of course, he fills me in on any relevant information, such as the president sending out discreet task forces to search for us. But he manages to talk about everything and nothing at the same time, alternating between the chaos of our situation and the comfort of normalcy in a way that helps regulate the temperature of the situation. I've become much closer to him over the past few weeks.

Our time away has also given me the opportunity to work on my skills. Night Walking, as I call it—to Amelia's chagrin—is becoming easier and easier. I'm now able to infiltrate minds without the consciousness I'm inhabiting noticing my presence. I've also successfully Shadowed—that's what I'm calling it when I'm present in a person's mind in real-time—several times without revealing myself.

Meeting other vampires has also been a wonderful experience. Granted, I'd prefer it if we weren't on the run from the federal government and needing help from them, but what can you do? It is what it is. Well, that's what I keep repeating to myself.

But, I know, once we meet up with the rest of the Loch clan, I will have the opportunity to work through my feelings and experiences. And considering we have just stepped foot on American soil, I'd say we are only a few moves away from making that our reality.

Jeremy seems like a nice guy. Mohan told me he's worked on the Border Patrol task force for eleven years. He's been instrumental in helping vampires cross into the US for most of the time he's worked there. His mission is clear. Pick us up and get us to the safe house. I'm not worried. My concern now is on Ricco and Paula.

Jeremy assures me we will be at the house in less than an hour, leaving us plenty of time before Ricco will begin his change. True to his word, we arrive at a large house, walled off from the outside world just under an hour later.

"Mohan has had the fridge stocked, and beds made," Jeremy says as we stop outside the front door. "It's one of his many houses."

I could roll my eyes. Mohan has arranged for us to stay in one of his most luxurious homes, which, considering the need to keep a low profile, is anything but discreet! Amusement overwhelms my slight irritation when I see the look on Paula and Ricco's faces. Horatio and Emilio tense slightly. I might not have Amelia's gift with senses, but even I can hear the rapid increase of their heartbeats.

Amelia looks far too tense. I haven't seen her relax for one day since this shitshow started. Maybe I can finally get her to unwind for a day or two before we're smuggled to see the family. In an ideal situation, I would seduce her, then claim her body until she couldn't walk, let alone worry. But it isn't just our new travel companions that make that scenario unlikely. It's Amelia's inability to let go long enough for me to successfully coax her into lovemaking.

Honestly, that could be half her issue. She's sex depressed. Hell, I know I am. Amelia's stress and anxiety are seriously messing with our bedroom antics. I'm well aware we have plenty to worry about and sex shouldn't be at the forefront of my mind, but it has practical benefits too. Amelia and I are passionate. We are never stronger than when we connect, both physically and emotionally. But so far, Amelia has put a stop to it every time I have tried to initiate something.

Jeremy interrupts my musings by clearing his throat. Amelia is looking at me with a knowing gaze. I stare back defiantly. We've never kept our feelings from one another, and I'm not about to start now. She looks away first, with anxiety etched across her beautiful face.

"You will only see me again if there is a problem," Jeremy says. "There is no reason for any issues to arrive, but here is an emergency remote, should you need to signal me." He hands me a small one-button remote control. "Just press the button and I will be here in minutes. There is also a panic room off the master bedroom. Mohan assures me he will guide you through everything." Jeremy is only talking to me now. Presumably, Jeremy knows I can communicate with Mohan.

Resting my hand on his forearm, I smile. "Thank you, Jeremy. For everything. We appreciate you."

Bowing his head ever so slightly, he smiles. "It is truly my honor." And with that, he turns and leaves.

We watch collectively as the clock strikes midnight. All eyes turn to Ricco, who closes his eyes and breathes in heavily. There is no dramatic change. Ricco won't flail around while his body goes through the change. But he will know, as will Amelia. She will feel Paula's soul reaching out for her mate.

Ricco and Paula sit together, holding hands. Paula's head rests on his shoulder. We all stay silent for what seems like an eternity until I notice a slight shift in Amelia's aura. It's like I can see her "other side" begin to stir. The deep blue of her life force brightens, and her eyes lock on Paula. Knowing what's coming, I slip from my seat and approach Emilio and Horatio, who look up at me with concern.

"It's time for us to leave," I say quietly.

Considering Amelia and I have been out of touch with everyone, we no longer have the luxury of having the new family doctor milk us for the serum we produce. That means she will be turning Paula the old-fashioned way, and that isn't something for the family to witness. Truth be told, I dislike watching it. Amelia gets violently sick every time human blood enters her stomach, which makes me ache for her.

Horatio wants to argue, but I level him with a stern look. It's the one I perfected behind the bar at Insomnia when a punter was dancing on the end of my last nerve. Emilio takes his husband by the hand and leads him out of the room. I take one last look at Amelia, who is laser focused on Paula, before retreating to the room we picked.

There is no need for me to insert myself into Emilio and Horatio's space. They will support each other. I need to check-in with Mohan and then gear myself up to receive Amelia.

I'm just saying goodbye to Mohan when I feel Amelia's rage run through me like ice. Her anger is not directed at Paula, but rather at life for allowing a vampire to fall in love with a human. Amelia is the one who feels their pain the most. She experiences what it's like for two fated souls to be kept apart by biology. And it's not just this one time, but every time she is near a vampire and their human mate.

However, now I know she is turning Paula. The spike in anger occurs as she is about to bite into human flesh. I wish we had a way to milk her. At least she gets a reprieve from having to be so close to such heartache and pain that way.

Thank the universe we were able to help Ricco and Paula so quickly. Amelia feels so much worse when she helps a human change whose mate is a Fallen. The longer they have been kept apart, the worse for Amelia. The human doesn't go unscathed either. Unlike the physical symptoms a vampire exhibits when kept from their mate, humans feel it emotionally. Like a deep depression. Cruel and unrelenting.

I slip into the shower and wash quickly. I want to cleanse myself of the past few weeks. Tonight, I will take steps to get us back on track as a couple. We might be anointed or whatever, but Amelia is still my wife. And I miss her.

My back has just hit the headboard when our door opens and Amelia slips in. She gives me a small smile before heading to the shower. I know she wants the hot water to cleanse away everything that's happened today and over the past few days, just like I did.

I wait patiently, trying to decide if I should attempt to seduce her or not. I'm warring with myself constantly, and frankly, it's pissing me off. When Amelia steps into the bedroom naked, my mind is made up. We have a lifetime together, and I do not intend to waste a second of it. This shit with the president will be here in the morning. It's not something that will simply disappear, and I cannot go without Amelia's touch indefinitely. Our souls are joined. When we are not together, I feel as if a part of me is physically missing. All the stress, fear, and anxiety become so big that they feel insurmountable. I know Amelia feels the same.

She approaches the bed, and I can see her mind is elsewhere. She's thinking about all the things that could go wrong before we reunite with the family. Drawing up to my knees, I reach forward, taking her hand, which snaps her back to the present.

"Erin," she begins, but I stop any more words from spilling out with two fingers pressed to her lips. My other hand rests over her heart as I simply look at my beautiful wife.

"Are Paula and Ricco okay?" She nods. "Good, then tonight is about us," I say, trailing my fingers from her lips to the back of her head. I pull her in and inhale her scent deeply. Our lips are millimeters apart and I know she is about to protest, so I stop. My breath spills over her mouth, and my eyes bore into hers. I open my mind entirely, flooding us both with my thoughts and feelings. I want Amelia to understand how much I miss her. How lost I feel when she steps back from my touch.

The emotional dump must work because she surges forward and takes my mouth in hers. The kiss is demanding and unapologetic, which I love.

Three

AMELIA

Keeping my distance—emotionally and physically—from Erin wasn't necessarily a conscious decision. I think a part of me threw up some walls to protect myself from letting fear consume me. Watching my life change without an ounce of control broke something within me.

We were crafting a life together. One that is supposed to be safe and surrounded by love. A life that is now being torn to pieces because of human ignorance. The same ignorance that has plagued this planet since the dawn of civilization.

The walls were only supposed to be temporary. Just until I got Erin safely out of Hawaii. But as the days passed, my walls grew higher, and the distance between us grew wider. Erin has tried many times to coax me into lovemaking, but every time, I nearly drown in anxiety. A voice haunts my subconscious, reminding me never to let the walls down. Not if I wanted to keep Erin safe and get us home. Now, I spend every waking moment consumed by fruitless planning. It's useless because I have zero clue where to even start. How do you take on the President of the United States? Vampires can fight, but we are peaceful at our core. We dedicate our lives to the prosperity of not just our kind, but humans as well.

In my darker moments, I wish we *were* made like the beasts in human fairytales. At least then I would feel like we have a fighting chance.

The distance I've put between Erin and me is counterintuitive. I know that. As we've established many times before, we are the strongest when we are close. So, by pulling us apart emotionally, I've weakened us. But it isn't something I've been able to control. My life is turning and turning, and I can't do a damn thing to stop it.

I need to get Erin to safety. I need to hold my family in my arms. I need to make sure I never lose control of myself like I did with Mack. So many things I need to do, and not a clue how to do them. Except for closing myself off and buckling down.

But now Erin has opened her mind and heart to me, flooding my senses with her heartache. My absence has hurt her, and I'll never forgive myself. In my quest to save us both, I have cast her to one side. Rejected her advances, when all she wanted to do was increase our bond by loving me.

I wanted to push her away again when I walked into the bedroom after my shower. Turning Paula left me feeling tainted. Not something I want anywhere near Erin, but then she pressed her fingers to my lips and the only thing I wanted to do was kiss her. So, I did.

I am.

Her skin is an angel's caress. Just the ghost of a touch sends my senses into overdrive. Our kiss is fierce as our hands grapple for skin. There is no entity on this earth more beautiful than Erin. Her soul glows golden as it breaks through my mental barrier. I can't stop the smile from taking over my face as I witness our soul colors unite.

Erin shifts, pulling me down on top of her. My body slides into its rightful place. Her pleasure is already coating her thighs. I need to consume every drop of it, but her grip remains strong. Her thighs clamp me in place.

"Not yet," she gasps as I rock into her.

I love eating her out. It's my favorite thing to do, whether I'm nestled between her legs or she's sitting on my face. But for Erin, it's the face-to-face orgasm she craves. She loves to witness my blue aura spark in my eyes as we join.

Pulling back, I give her what she wants. Unrestricted access to all that I am. Her irises illuminate. Bright gold rings stare back at me as I snake my hand between us. Our colors dance and entwine, shrouding us from the outside world. Our panting spurs me on. I love to hear her excitement and anticipation.

"Please don't tease me. Not today." She whimpers as I gently run the tip of my finger over her clit.

Instead of answering, I press two fingers inside. She's tight and warm. Her muscles contract instantly. I want her to give me all she has, so I quickly slip in a third finger and thrust. My own sex is pulsing with need. Erin grabs my ass, pulling me closer, causing my pussy to bear down on her thigh.

We are rushing toward a glorious crescendo, and I berate myself for ever keeping Erin at bay. My scream escapes my throat as the most glorious climax washes over me. My hand has stilled inside Erin, but it doesn't matter. She has her head thrown back, and her own scream echoes around the room. It will take many more moments like this until we are sated.

The cicadas sing as we lay sweating from head to toe. We should shower, but the fragrance of sex is the reminder of our night together. A reminder I need to keep at the forefront of my mind for a few hours more.

"Can you feel it, my love?" Erin murmurs. Her lips trace my jaw. "The raw power."

"Yes," I moan, as her fingers twist my nipple.

"I want you one more time," she whispers. "But this will be purely for my pleasure."

I'm turned on to my stomach. My hands instinctively grip the pillow. Erin shifts off the bed and goes to our luggage. My eyes are closed but I hear exactly what she retrieves. My heart rate spikes, and I feel her smiling with her whole being.

The bed dips. My knees are parted. "Your body is worthy of worship." Her hands caress the back of my legs until she reaches my ass. She playfully smacks it, making my clit ache. "Oh baby, your clit will have to wait its turn."

God, she drives me wild when she reads me like that.

Hooking her hands under my hips, she draws them up. My head remains buried in the pillow, waiting. Waiting for what she's about to do to me. A cold, wet sensation trickles between my cheeks. I shiver. Erin hasn't stopped touching me and I'm about to lose my mind. She's an expert at edging me.

The tip of her dildo swipes through my folds, coating my pussy in lube. Erin pushes in, stretching me wide. She is impatient.

My moan is guttural. She wastes no time picking up speed. Her rhythm is fast and deep. I can feel every inch of her, and I want more. She plucks my thoughts from my head the second they form.

One hand remains on my hip as the other traces my spine with the object I crave the most. I'm already close to the edge when her hand reaches the bottom of my back. She continues lower until I feel the sweet pressure of the other toy pushing against my asshole. Erin is going to fill me entirely.

Relaxing as best I can, I whimper in sheer delight as she pushes the plug into me. The pressure of the dildo and butt plug inside me violently throws me off the cliff one last time. I know I'm making a mess, but I'm too delirious with pleasure to really care.

Only when my body collapses to the bed do I come back to reality. Erin pulls out of me slowly but leaves the plug in, just the way I like it. She's so in tune with my every need. When the last vestiges of my orgasm are nearly gone, Erin slowly pulls the plug from me. I give one last gasp before I fall into a deep and sated sleep.

Compared to the weight it held before last night, the heaviness I've felt over the past two weeks is now just a shadow of itself. My heart is open and content. With her hand placed over it, Erin softly whispers words of love.

"Rest," she says. "We still have a few more hours until we're needed."

I shift, rolling onto my side so our faces are only centimeters apart. "I'm sorry, Erin."

She shakes her head. "It's been hard. I know." I go to protest because Erin is letting me off far too easily. "I accept your apology. Okay?"

"I've pushed you away."

"Yes. But now we're together again. Your heart is open."

I take a deep breath. "I feel like everything is spinning out of control. Getting home is just the beginning, Erin. What then? How do we put this genie back in its bottle?"

Her hand palms my face. "I don't know. All we can do is take things one day at a time. This isn't all on our shoulders, Amelia. We will have the vampire community on our side. We'll figure something out."

"How do you calm me so easily?"

She smiles. "Not so easily if the past two weeks are anything to go by. But I know your head isn't solely filled with thoughts of our current predicament. You've been struggling since Mack."

"I replay it over and over again, Erin. The urge to bite Mack. I had no control. I had to be wrestled to the floor."

"But you can control it now. You have done every day since."

"Yes, until the day I can't." It's my greatest fear, outside of Erin getting hurt.

Erin sits up on her elbow. I brush my fingers through her silky hair. "Is it any easier now?"

I nod. "Yes. But that scares me. I don't want to let my guard down. All it would take is a bite too deep, or a blood draw too long, and I could kill someone." She studies my face. I appreciate the fact she isn't trying to read my thoughts. Allowing me the space to talk on my own terms. "The side of me that feels the injustice that nature has put upon these people turns me almost feral. Like I have to take every drop of their blood before they are cured of their curse."

"I had no idea," she says into my mouth as she gently kisses me.

"It's my burden to bear. You have your own changes to deal with. Although, I think it's safe to say you're a natural. A true Queen." I smile.

"No, I have it easier." Something else that has evolved since the first time Erin encountered a Fallen. She can block their pain and suffering now. I know she sees their dimmed light, but that's all. Erin doesn't have to go through the heartache I do. "Amelia, I'm here. Your burden, my burden, it doesn't matter. We deal with it all as one. I won't let you lose control, honey. I promise."

My lips seek hers again. We kiss until all our troubles are a mere wisp of a memory. Erin fills my mind entirely.

"All being well, we'll see the family tonight," I say, hoping the topic of our family will help me absorb some positivity. I'm tired of everything feeling so dark.

"Nothing will go wrong," Erin soothes. "Mohan has everything prepared. Now kiss me again, and then we'll get up. I want to check on Ricco and Paula."

"It worked. Paula has changed."

I'm just glad that Erin didn't need to intervene. We've discovered that Erin isn't necessary if the mate of a potential Fallen turns close to the same time as their loved one. It's fortunate Paula is already over thirty. They won't have to wait to start their immortal life together. Not like some we've encountered who have waited years for their human mate to reach an age where the transformation can be completed. Like Erin and me. The waiting is the hardest part.

Erin smiles. "Be proud, Amelia. Ricco and Paula have a future because of you."

I shake my head. "They should never have had to worry, Erin. I just don't understand why we are made this way. Why would the universe create us to be deeply loving creatures? Soul searchers? And then make it so we can't be with the one that calls to us. It's so unbelievably cruel."

Erin pulls me close. "It's no different from the injustices of the human world. We just have to work with what we've got. And for vampires, they have us. A light in the dark. There is still so much for us to learn. Who knows, maybe others will develop similar gifts to ours."

"Maybe." I sigh. "Or maybe we're it."

"And if that's true. We'll do everything in our power to help as many as possible."

"While being hunted by the president's attack dogs?"

"Yes," Erin states. "Because the Fallen and their mates are worth the risk of getting caught. But as I said. We have a lot of people behind us. I have faith in the council, in our community."

"What if it's all-out war?" I ask.

It's Erin's turn to shake her head. "That's not the vampire way."

"But it *is* the human way."

Four

ERIN

Begrudgingly, I agree to shower and head downstairs to eat. After last night, I was more than happy to ask Jeremy to postpone the trip for another twenty-four hours. My libido is far from satisfied. But Amelia made some good points about getting to safety and she also gave me another two orgasms in the shower.

The kitchen is alive with laughter when Amelia and I walk in. It makes my heart happy to see Ricco and Paula snuggled in each other's arms by the breakfast bar. Paula is almost at the end of her change. But I can feel their souls have bonded. There is a pureness to their energy. They are utterly content and they make a beautiful family. Emilio spots us first. His eyes are glassy and his smile wide. "Thank you," he cries.

Amelia tenses as she's hauled into a hug. Emilio's tears soak through Amelia's silk shirt. She looks like a deer in headlights, which makes me chuckle.

"Um…you're welcome," she squeaks. Her eyes are pleading with me. I don't need to read her mind to know she wants me to rescue her.

"Honey, let her go." Horatio laughs, stepping from behind the breakfast bar. Pulling his husband off a stunned Amelia, he turns to me and sinks to one knee. His head bowed. "We are in your debt once again."

"There is no debt," I say, looking at Amelia, who smiles. "We are honored to help."

"That may be so," Emilio says, wiping away his tears. "But you saved our boy from a fate worse than death. They will live happily together, because of you both. And we all know the risk you took to do it."

"What have you heard?" Amelia asks, breaking away to grab us both a coffee.

Horatio goes back to the stove and begins adding pancake batter to a pan. Emilio sits on a free bar stool. "We started hearing whispers. Just rumors, we thought. After the council spread word about your ascension, more vampires joined in wanting our identities to be revealed. The movement was picking up speed. We even heard the Grand Master was onboard."

"And then nothing," Ricco adds. "Suddenly vampires were leaving, going underground."

"The big family names," Emilio said. "The Loch's for one. The Grand Master vanished into thin air."

"And then a different set of rumors started. Ones saying that vampires were being hunted down," Horatio interjects. "Just over the span of two days, nearly every vampire in our community became aware that something was very wrong and that you both had been attacked."

"It was hard to tell what was fact and fiction," Paula says. "But with so much uncertainty, we decided to leave."

Ricco kisses Paula on her head before speaking. "But with my birthday so close, my fathers didn't want to leave anything to chance. I'm an ex-Army Ranger, so I put my skills to good use and tracked you both."

"We know it was selfish of us," Horatio says. His eyes cast downward.

"We've seen the pain and suffering the Fallen endure. Not to mention the anguish their mate has to experience. Please don't feel bad about wanting to keep your family from going through that," Amelia replies. Failing to mention that she, herself, experiences the horror and pain. She may not have Fallen, but Amelia knows torment.

"The Grand Master informed the president of our existence, and it didn't go how we hoped," I say jovially.

Amelia rolls her eyes. *That's an understatement*, she thinks. "It's true we were attacked. Erin has managed to stay in contact with the Grand Master, but we need to get back to our family."

"And that's where I come in," Jeremy calls as he enters the kitchen. "We need to leave within the hour."

"Where are we going?" I ask.

"Nevada. We have a long drive."

Emilio begins cleaning the kitchen. "You three get going. We will clean up and leave the house in a couple of hours, if that's okay?"

"You're not coming with us?" Amelia asks. Her link to Paula will still be thrumming through her veins.

"We know you have bigger things to think about," Ricco begins, but I hold my hand up again.

"Please come with us. We have no idea who is being targeted. I would feel better if you stayed close."

We need to stick together. Of that I am certain.

The family share a few looks before Horatio nods. "Thank you. We appreciate the offer."

"Okay," Jeremy claps. "Let's get this show on the road."

We're out of the house within thirty minutes, a testament to how badly we all want to feel some semblance of safety. Jeremy tells us Mohan has sent word for all the Grand Masters, council members, and elders to meet. They should be congregated by the time we arrive. I've tried to reach out to him, because I'm not sure gathering all our leaders in one spot is a good plan, but he's blocking me out.

Amelia squeezes my hand. We're sitting silently in the back of the SUV. Emilio and Horatio are in front of us, chatting quietly. Ricco and Paula are asleep. Although we practically ran out of the house this morning, I'm still feeling quite relaxed. Bonding with Amelia last night healed the rift all this chaos has caused. I know there will still be times when Amelia struggles to accept herself and will worry about losing control. But I will do everything I can to make her see she's not the monster she fears.

"I enjoyed last night," she mumbles.

"Mmm, it was rather nice, wasn't it?" I love the flash of indignation that crosses her face. She's so easy to tease.

"Nice?" She chuckles.

I look at her through heavy lashes and a sultry grin. "Very nice?"

Letting out a bark of laughter, she takes my chin between her forefinger and thumb. "Yes, it was *very* nice." She kisses me with so much passion I'm ready to drop my panties for her, here and now.

"You can't kiss me like that. Not when you can't finish what you start." I murmur into her mouth.

I flood my thong the second I see that glint in her eye that tells me she accepts the challenge. Her hand snakes to the top of my thigh but goes no further. Her eyes stay locked on me, and that's when I feel the shimmer of her want wash over my entire body. She's going to make me come without touching me. I can't help but bite my lip in anticipation. It's like a fire has been lit in her, and I love it.

She quickly checks on our companions. They are either unaware or pretending not to notice. I don't care either way. The risk makes it more fun.

Her thoughts are pure eroticism. She's picturing all the things she wants to do to me. My breathing catches as a vivid image sears into my mind of Amelia unbuckling her belt and sliding out our shared favorite toy. I see myself straddling her in the back of the SUV. She takes the head and rubs it through my growing wetness. I lower myself until I'm stretched and taking every inch. Amelia wraps her hand in my hair and pulls, exposing my throat.

I know this isn't really happening, but I can't stop my fangs from revealing themselves. Amelia knows I love it when we share blood in the throes of fucking. The first time we did it, we shocked ourselves. It was entirely instinctual.

Usually, we don't bite unless we are deprived of each other, which is why I'm yearning for it now. The sex last night was just the beginning. We will both need a lot more time together to fulfill our thirst.

Closing my eyes, I lose myself in the fantasy Amelia is creating for us. I'm riding her slowly as she sinks her teeth into my neck. The toy plunges deep inside until the timer runs out and it begins to vibrate.

Keep quiet, my love.

Yes, I must stay quiet. We are in a car full of vampires who see us as royalty. We're not being very regal right now. Which, if I'm honest, adds to the excitement.

My pussy contracts even though there is no toy inside me. I'm going to climax, and there is not a damn thing I can do—or want to do—to stop it. Her hand tightens on my thigh. A warning to remain silent. Which I do. In my head, however, I am screaming in sheer delight as I come all over her.

My eyes flicker open as the rush of my orgasm recedes. Amelia is watching me with a cocky grin on her face. I flick a look at the other passengers, who are none the wiser of what she has just done to me. The only proof is my ruined underwear and my heavy breathing. Running the tips of my fingers over the spot on my neck where fantasy Amelia bit down, I have to stop myself from groaning in disappointment. How I wish I could act out Amelia's thoughts this instant. God, what I wouldn't do to make her scream.

As real as she made it feel, nothing will beat her hands on me. But for now, I will have to bathe in the afterglow of Amelia's fantastic mind fuck.

Licking my lips, I lift my hips and slide my underwear down. Amelia tracks my every movement. Her nose flares as I slip the garment into her hand.

"Good job, baby," I whisper.

Life almost feels normal as we cruise along. These few hours of respite have helped reset my equilibrium. Now Amelia and I have connected properly, and several times, I have a clarity of mind that has been absent for the past few weeks.

"Ten minutes," Jeremy calls. When I heard Nevada, I was expecting the desert for some reason. I guessed having a secret lair or something would go well with Area 51. However, we have entered Humboldt-Toiyabe National Forest and are heading off road toward the mountains.

"Secret lair?" Amelia asks with adorably scrunched eyebrows.

Shrugging, I nod. "Well, yeah. It feels like the situation calls for a secret lair."

She titters but says no more. We are close and her nerves are sky high. Amelia is almost vibrating as Jeremy pulls the car into a long driveway. Tall firs tower above us. We are completely secluded.

It's another three minutes until we stop outside a log cabin. It doesn't look big enough to fit a single vampire comfortably, let alone dozens. The building is nothing like the mansion we spent the night in. Amelia holds my hands as we wait for Jeremy to unload the back. Emilio, Horatio, Ricco, and Paula fall behind us.

The inside of the cabin is as basic as the outside, and empty. I feel Amelia flex. She's getting agitated. I fill her mind with calming thoughts.

"Follow me," Jeremy says, leading us through to a bedroom. He moves a single bed out of the way, revealing an opening in the floor. *Ha! Secret lair, I knew it.*

"Cool," Ricco mutters.

"Well, the cabin makes sense now." I laugh. Amelia is already moving and stepping down the stairs.

We step onto a concrete floor. Jeremy bids us goodbye and covers the entrance. Overhead halogens automatically turn on, lighting the way. Striding with confident steps, Amelia leads us forward. We walk until we come to a steel door. There is no handle. I want to make a comment about how very *Underworld* this is feeling, but I don't think Amelia would appreciate it.

She raises her hand to knock, but the door swings open and Amelia is pulled into the arms of Victoria Loch. My smile hasn't even fully formed before I am dragged into the fold. Harlan holds us all in his arms.

We made it.

Five

AMELIA

I feel as if I am floating. My mother's arms are a balm to my frayed nerves. Her scent simultaneously comforts and breaks me. I feel the rush of tears streak down my face as she holds me tight. More bodies move around us, and I feel my father's towering presence as he holds Mother, myself, and Erin.

Erin is just as relieved as me. Our souls tingle with anticipated happiness. We made it. Our family is safe.

"Oh, my darlings. I am so happy to have you back with us," Mother whispers, her voice thick with emotion. I'm unable to talk. My voice refuses to come. Gripping her tighter, I pour all my feelings into her.

"Is everyone okay?" Erin asks.

"All fine, don't worry," Father answers. It's another couple of minutes before I feel safe to step back. Holding my mother at arm's length, I survey her, needing to see for my own eyes. They really are okay.

Neither my mother nor father have a hair out of place. They look as cool and collected as usual. There is a ruckus of noise as the rest of our clan push through the considerable crowd. Erin and I are swept up into the arms of my siblings. Lucille stands back, waiting for her turn. Throughout our lives, Lucille and I have always been volatile toward one another. We just seem to rub each other up the wrong way. Since meeting Erin, our relationship has morphed into something different. We still irritate each other immensely, but now, I have a love so deep for her. She gives me shit, but she has shown herself to be the most loyal and loving sibling out of the entire clan.

Stepping back from Aliah, I stand in front of Lucille. We regard each other for a few moments before moving into each other's arms. "You asshole," she hisses into my ear, causing me to laugh.

"I missed you too, Luce."

We finally break away and wipe our faces. I'm filled with so much love. Erin takes my hand and nuzzles my cheek. "We're going to be okay, honey," she murmurs.

"Hello," my mother says, speaking to Horatio.

Stepping forward, I lay my hand on Horatio's shoulder. "Oh, yes, sorry, let me introduce you to Horatio and his husband, Emilio. Ricco, their son, and Paula, his mate."

"It's a pleasure to meet you all," Horatio replies, bowing slightly.

"We met up with them before crossing the border," Erin supplies.

"Yes, their majesties were kind enough to help our son and Paula."

I hear Lucille snigger at the use of our formal titles—that, I may add—I did not agree to!

"Ricco turned thirty last night," I say.

"And you helped Paula," my mother replies, not really asking. I nod. She squeezes my hand. It's a strange thing to get recognition for biting a human. It doesn't sit well with me, no matter how many times Erin tries to convince me I'm a good person. I still have to consume human blood. I vomit as much as I can, but a small part absorbs into my system. It's how my bond with the human lasts.

"Welcome. Please make yourselves at home. There is Red in the next room and enough food to feed an army. Bedrooms further along," Father says, shaking hands with Emilio and the rest of the family.

Mother turns to Erin and me. "Erin, your parents are here. Kit and Claire too."

"Where is Mohan?" Erin asks. I know she is desperate to see her parents, but we must speak to Mohan. There is much we have missed, and although they have communicated, I'm positive there is a lot he has kept to himself.

"In the office," Mother answers.

"What is this place?" I ask. The bunker is huge. Even though it is filled with dozens upon dozens of vampires, there is still ample room. I can see doors branching off to different parts. I wonder just how deep the structure runs.

Marcus, one of my older siblings, grins. "Another of Mohan's real estate purchases. The man has properties everywhere. It's quite impressive."

"Harlan, would you mind showing us to the office?" Erin says before turning to Mother. "Victoria, would you let my parents know we are here and will be with them as soon as possible, but the meeting with Mohan cannot wait."

"Of course, take your time. They understand."

Father gestures for us to follow. As we move, the crowd parts. Every single head bows in our presence.

"Christ," I hiss just loud enough for Erin to hear. She smiles at the people, ignoring me.

"Oh, thank the universe," Mohan cries the second we enter the office. "You don't know how happy I am to see you both, and how so very sorry I am. This is all my doing," he blurts. I think he's on the verge of tears.

"Mohan, please," Erin begins, but the Grand Master shakes his head.

"I went into the meeting far too excited, Your Majesty. I'd barely said the word vampire before I was telling the president about our new queens. It's my fault."

I've done my best not to place blame. After all, we knew revealing ourselves posed a considerable risk. However, I can't help but growl in frustration at Mohan's utter lack of precaution. His naivety is astounding. We told him not to even utter the words savior queen. Not until we knew how things would unravel. He didn't listen.

My growl must have been audible because Mohan drops to his knees in front of me. Erin places her hand on my arm, looking at me with concern.

"Amelia, it isn't on Mohan. The president didn't waste a second deciding we are a threat."

"I am aware," I grind out. "But maybe if the Grand Master had used some common sense, instead of verbally vomiting, we wouldn't have been attacked in our bed! Maybe if he'd listened to us, we wouldn't have spent two weeks clawing our way home!"

"I am so sorry, so sorry," Mohan cries, and this time I see tears.

"Tell us exactly what happened. Do not skip a word," I bark. Maybe I should be calmer and willing to forgive him, but his excitement put my mate in danger.

Erin helps Mohan to his feet. She's pissed at me, which is just wonderful. We've only just got back in balance with each other and now I am in the doghouse.

Knowing I need some space, I take a few steps back and lean against the wall as Erin sits with Mohan. He tells us about his meeting. How he barely made it out of the White House without being arrested.

"I contacted you the second I was out of danger," he says to Erin. "I contacted as many council members as possible to start the evacuation. I knew the president would begin her search for anyone linked to me."

"And how *exactly* did she deduce Erin is the queen?" It's one thing he revealed a new vampire queen. It's something else if he told the president who the queen and her mate are by name.

Mohan pales. "I mentioned your first names. Nothing more, but that must have been enough."

Anger boils in my blood. I don't care that he is our elected leader. I want to hurt him for putting Erin in harm's way. A wash of calm penetrates my mind. Erin is trying to help me, but it isn't enough. I need to leave, to get away from him, so I can calm down.

Pushing off the wall, I leave the office. Father and Laurence are waiting outside. I see their concern as I storm past them, searching for a place that isn't occupied.

"In here," Lucille says, grabbing my arm and dragging me into a small bedroom. "This room is reserved for you and Erin, so no one is allowed in."

"You're in it," I snap.

"To save you from doing or saying something stupid, you moron," she retorts with venom.

"Fuck you, Lucille."

A malicious grin spreads across her face. "Ah, you want a fight," she sneers. "That can be arranged. Follow me." She rips the door open, causing people to look. My anger is still too prominent to care what others are thinking. Lucille is right. I *do* want a fight.

She leads me to a gym. This place is ridiculous. The room is fully kitted out and has enough space for a sparing ring. Lucille climbs in, forgoing any hand wraps or body protection which is fine by me.

I jump from the doorway and land in the ring. I see the look of surprise on Lucille's face, which makes me grin. We haven't fought in a long time. I've changed a lot.

"Let's go," I growl.

"Fight like a Loch, not a queen. None of your fancy new skills. Let's see if you can take me the old-fashioned way," she taunts me as we begin.

We circle each other. Lucille was a better fighter than me. But I always gave as good as I got, which I intend to do now. I'll fight like a Loch. I'll fight with all the rage I've pent up for weeks.

We clash in a haze of fists and feet. We are both proficient in mixed martial arts. Lucille lands several punches, almost knocking me to the mat.

"You've been training." I wipe a drop of blood from my lip.

"I never stopped training, sister."

We go round after round. My anger filtering out through every punch until I am a sweaty mess on the floor. Lucille lays next to me heaving a breath as we starfish, looking up to the concrete ceiling.

"You're a good sister," I pant out.

"I know," she replies. "You've gotten stronger."

"I know."

Lucille rolls to her side. "Still want to rip Mohan's head off?"

I lick my lips. "Yes, but at least I feel in control now."

"He was wrong. He hasn't shied away from owning his mistake. We know he fucked up, Amelia. Now we have to work out how to move forward. You need to work out how to move forward *with* him."

"I know."

"I bet Erin has already forgiven him." Rolling to her back again.

I scoff. "Erin didn't blame him in the first place."

Lucille grins. "I'm sure she didn't."

We fall silent for a few seconds. "This new side of me, the one born to protect the queen, is a strong force, Luce. I'm not even sure Erin fully understands how powerful it is. The mere hint of a threat toward her and I am compelled to leave the earth in flaming ruins to protect her."

"Dramatic." She chuckles, which makes me smile.

"Maybe so, but it's true. I'm still learning how to live with it."

"You make it sound as if it isn't you. Amelia, this 'other side' you keep referring to isn't a separate entity. It is *you*. Erin's transformation into the Salvator Regina comes from within her biology. I know we're working from prophecies and all that shit. But this is real. Your bond has unleashed a change in both of your DNA. That isn't magic. It's evolution. You *are* this protective side. Once you embrace it, you will control it."

"I can't accept being a monster," I sob. "The anger is all-consuming at times, Luce."

"Don't be so fucking ridiculous. You are no monster. But you are being an asshole. Erin needs you to get a goddamn grip. There is a reason the queen needs her protector. Together, you make a whole. Together, you are saving our kind from hell. Stop feeling sorry for yourself and do your job."

Lucille hauls herself up and leaves the gym. She always knew how to make a statement. And a dramatic exit.

The silence envelops me. Closing my eyes, I meditate. Before we were attacked, I'd gotten good at clearing my mind. Meditation was helping me deal with all the upheaval. Lucille is harsh, but she may be right. I've been spiraling, and that doesn't help Erin. She's having to hold everything together, including me.

Centering my thoughts, I gather all my feelings. Anger is still the strongest emotion, but I also feel fear, anxiety, and love. Concentrating, I pull the love forward. Ignoring or pushing away any emotion only leads to disaster, but that doesn't mean I have to let it take up too much room inside. I acknowledge my anger is still there but allow love to bloom larger. I summon other emotions forward, such as happiness and calm. Instead of fighting myself, I have to make peace.

I can view my calling to protect the queen as something to be feared, or I can let it fill me with pride. Acceptance isn't easy, but I know I have to accomplish it—for the sake of my mate and community. I also have to have faith that as my partner in all things, Erin will be there to pull me back if I ever overstep.

$\mathcal{S}ix$

ERIN

Watching Amelia storm out of the room and not follow is hard and heartbreaking. She is my mate. When Amelia hurts, I hurt. And right now, she is in pain. Just the thought of me getting hurt sends a visceral pain through her body. I feel it. But I know she needs time to cool down, and I need to reassure Mohan. The community needs him to be a strong leader, so falling apart is out of the question.

"I'm sorry, Erin," he repeats. "I took a golden opportunity and ruined it."

I stroke his back. He is more than the Grand Master to me. We are friends, and I truly dislike seeing my friends suffer. Yes, okay, he was foolish to blurt out the things he did, but I know it came from a place of optimism. After so many years of watching his people suffer, he was given hope. Unfortunately, that hope meant nothing to the president. All she heard were the words "vampires" and "the risen queen." Of course, she panicked. It's probably ingrained in the human genome to panic and then obliterate.

But what's done is done.

Now, I have to focus on stopping the annihilation of our people. It's not lost on me how much closer I feel to vampires than I ever did to humans. Maybe I took being part of a community for granted when I was human. Yet, when I think about the differences between our species, they seem profound.

As a human, I cherished life and shared it with friends and family. But as a vampire, I love more fiercely, more deeply. My friends and family are not just in my life—they are a *part* of me. Everything I feel is deeper, somehow magnified, in this new form. With absolute certainty, I know that becoming a vampire was my destiny. And it's a destiny I will fight to defend with everything I have.

"My friend, you need to stop. There is too much work to be done for self-pity." I don't want to come across as harsh, but time is ticking. We have no idea what the president intends to do next.

Producing a handkerchief, Mohan wipes his face. He straightens up and takes my hand. "I will do whatever it takes to keep you all safe. You have my word."

I smile. "I know you will. Is that why you've called all these people here?"

He nods. "Yes. This is bigger than me. We need to decide as a community how to respond."

Suddenly, a wave of fury fogs my mind. Amelia is getting angrier. Concentrating, I do my best to connect with her. A sharp pain crashes against my face. "Shit," I hiss, bringing my fingers to my lips. No blood. What the hell is she doing?

"Erin?"

"I'm fine. It's Amelia."

Mohan stays quiet as I investigate. Closing my eyes, I force my way into her mind. She doesn't register my presence, as I now know she's far too busy pummeling Lucille.

"Sorry about that," I say, leaving Amelia's mind and returning to the office. "Everything is fine."

"She's never going to forgive me." He sighs, looking downcast.

"Yes, she will. Amelia is contending with a lot of emotions right now. Seeing her family will help."

"I hope so."

We take a few moments. There is a lot of emotion in this bunker. A powder keg if we're not careful.

Finally, I break the silence. "When do you plan on addressing them?"

"I was waiting for you to arrive."

"Give me some time to see my parents and catch up with the family." I'll need Amelia by my side for this, but she's still working out her aggression.

"Take all the time you need. I will do the rounds, keep everyone fed and happy until you're ready."

Mohan leaves first. I need a few minutes alone to collect myself. Along with the title of Salvator Regina comes the expectation that I can somehow fix everything. I know what Amelia and I can do is almost miraculous, and I'm grateful every day that we can do some good, but even we have limits. I think.

I'd hoped to have many, *many* years of settling into this role before having to face the masses as some sort of savior figure. I guess that's not an option anymore. Amelia and I are going to be thrust into the center of this. I just know it. Reality is, we're only helpful if more Fallen need helping. I've no special powers to stop a president from annihilating an entire species.

Before I do anything else, I need to see my parents. I can feel that Amelia is calmer, which is a relief. I'll thank Lucille later. If anyone can get Amelia to blow off steam, it's her. Preferably, I'd like it to involve less violence, but whatever works.

I slip out of the office, hoping to stay under the radar. No luck. It's like an alarm goes off as soon as I open the door. Time to be the queen they all want. Holding my head high, I walk through the crowd, smiling. I acknowledge as many people as I can until I finally spot my mom. She's rushing toward me, and I drop all decorum. I'm not the Salvator Regina, I'm Erin. A daughter who has been terrified of never seeing her family again.

"Come with me," my mom says, taking me by the waist. She leads me down a corridor to a small bedroom where my dad is waiting. We spend time hugging and crying. They are way past the whole vampire thing now. All they want is to see me happy and safe.

"Are you both okay?"

"Perfectly fine," Mom says. "We were whisked away with Victoria and the gang as soon as Mohan sent word."

"Where have you been?" Mohan never disclosed their location.

"We moved about quite a bit until we got here. It's a bit doomsday but it'll do," Dad jokes.

"What about you, sweetheart? How did your travels go?" I love how Mom phrases it. Like Amelia and I were gallivanting around, taking in the sights.

"It was tough. But we met a lot of good people along the way."

"Where is Amelia? We saw her storm off earlier. Did you have a fight? It must have been hard on you both!"

"No Mom, we aren't fighting. She's just stressed. It was hard for her to hear...the reason we were attacked."

"Yeah, I had a few words with the Grand Master myself." Dad huffs. "I'd thought he'd have known better than to go spilling names. Not like that."

"I know," I placate. "But placing blame is useless. If we start doing that, the only thing we will do is tear the community apart. Remember, there was a whole group of people who wanted the humans to know. We could place the blame there if we wanted. But there's no point."

"I know, sweetie," Dad says, a tear forming. "But he put my little girl in danger. It was tough to hear."

We hold each other for another minute until I feel Amelia reaching out to me. Pulling back, I tell them I need to find my mate. We need to get back to the level we were on this morning when she was making me come through thought alone in the back of a car.

Following her presence, I rush through the crowds until I find the door I'm looking for. Pushing into the room, I breathe easier as I see Amelia sitting on a bed, head in hands. She looks up, and I can see something has changed, shifted. The haunted look I've become accustomed to seeing is gone.

"I'm sorry," she begins. "I don't wish for us to fight, Erin."

"Me either. I know you're angry, my love, but you have to push past it. Blaming Mohan isn't the answer."

She sighs and nods. "I know. It took several rounds in the ring plus a verbal ass-whooping from Lucille to get through to me."

I laugh. "Should've known you needed your ass handed to you by Luce. Can't believe I didn't think of it sooner."

She playfully knocks my shoulder. "I'll talk to Mohan, I promise. But can I have a little more time to be pissed with him?" She grins.

"Fine, you get another ten minutes."

"That's specific." She chuckles.

"That's how long we have until Mohan addresses the folks out there." I point to the door. "He knows we need to come together and form a plan. It's going to take all of us to figure this one out."

Amelia brushes her fingers across my cheek. "Does he want you to speak?"

"What do you think?" I say it in jest, but Amelia knows I'm nervous. She remains silent as I gather my thoughts. "I'm scared, baby. They look at us as if we are Gods. I feel like I'm letting them down. There's nothing either of us can do to fix this for them. But how can we tell them that?"

"We don't," Amelia replies. "We talk and listen to them. If they're expecting a miracle, they will be disappointed. We haven't appointed ourselves as their saviors."

"You've seen how they react. They haven't needed us to tell them anything. They've made their minds up."

"And that's on them. We go out there and just be ourselves. Help where we can."

I crawl onto her lap and wrap my arms around her neck. "I'd give anything to be in the penthouse right now, or behind the bar serving asshole frat boys."

"And I'd give anything to be there watching you serve asshole frat boys. You know how sexy I find it when you're pulling pints?"

"Behave." I giggle.

Her hand snakes around my body until she's cupping my breast. "What if I don't want to, huh, Mrs. Loch?"

"Amelia," I say rather breathlessly.

She grins wolfishly and retracts her hand. "Okay, I'll behave...for now."

I know she only did that to take my mind off the group of keen vampires in the next room, and I love her for it. But we have to bite the bullet and get out there.

Taking my hand, Amelia leads me out. A silence befalls the room immediately, which, in all honesty, does not help my anxiety. Mohan stands on a chair on the other side of the room. He claps his hands three times. The acoustics down here are pretty impressive.

"Everyone, can I have your attention, please?"

He didn't really need to ask that. Every set of eyeballs is squarely on him now. Amelia guides me toward him, using the outer wall to skim around everyone. There are two more chairs standing by Mohan, presumably for Amelia and I. Taking a deep breath, I hoist myself up. Amelia immediately stands on the last chair, and predictably, they all drop to one knee and bow their heads.

"Oh, for...get up," Amelia barks. I can't help but roll my lips in to stop myself from laughing. She looks over at her family, who, apart from Lucille, are all on their knees.

Are they fucking serious? She growls.

My darling, please calm down.

Lucille rolls her eyes and flips Amelia the bird. Amelia laughs, dispelling her irritation. Slowly, the masses stand up and look at us expectantly. Is this where I'm supposed to make some sort of speech?

"I'd like to welcome you all again," Mohan calls. "I know it has been a troubling few weeks and you are all eager to get home. Before that can happen, we must discuss the next steps. I have spoken to their majesties, and we agree that a solution is only possible through talking to you all. This is bigger than one vampire. We are all in danger."

"We need to fight back," a voice from the back booms through the room. My eyes whip to the source, but whoever shouted it isn't as forthcoming now the spotlight is on them.

There is a murmur of agreement that ripples through the crowd. It's a dangerous thing. A crowd can easily turn into a mob. I don't know what to say. Mohan looks panicked. It's Amelia who holds her hand up, garnering all the attention.

She suddenly looks fierce. I'm not sure why it is happening in this instance, but I can see clearly her blue aura. I feel her, but it's not like when we are in the throes of passion. This is different. I am overwhelmed by the sense of protection Amelia is casting my way. I am seeing her "other side," her warrior.

Seven

AMELIA

The pressure Erin is putting on herself is immense, which is why it's my turn to bear some of the burden. She's had the weight of the world on her shoulders for far too long. Not only has she had to deal with her unforeseen transformation into a vampire and queen, but Erin has had to support me with unwavering confidence as I struggle to come to terms with this unknown part of myself. I should feel ashamed. But maybe it's a testament to my wife's character and strength. The reason she has become the Salvator Regina. I am in awe of her.

After Lucille's somewhat harsh pep talk and a little meditation, I am finally ready to take the reins from her for a little while. Time to step up and be what I was born to be. Erin's protector and queen consort. Which is why I put my hand up when the moron in the back shouted out his unhelpful comment. Erin blanched, and I could hear her thoughts racing, trying to come up with something to say.

Well, I have something to say. Though there is a crowd, the silence is deafening. I stand tall with my hand still in the air. I want every single eye on me. I feel the ancient protector in me rise. I feel my warrior surround me. Yes, I am ready now.

"You want to fight?" My voice is loud and commanding. There isn't a ripple of sound. "Mr. Becker?" The asshole thought he could call out and remain anonymous. I can hear his heart rate triple in speed. Idiot.

A few council members turn their attention to the young vampire, waiting for him to answer. My eyes bore into him from across the room. I can see his mind whirring, trying to decide what his next move should be. Finally, he holds himself a little taller. "What choice do we have? Our numbers are vast."

I'd like to smack him. The man has no idea. He's a privileged vampire that has never had to deal with anything in his comfortable life. I know privilege, but at least I work hard. Neither my family nor I take what we have for granted.

"Hmm, so you are ready to personally engage in armed combat and fight against the United States military?"

This fool doesn't know his ass from a hole in the ground.

"I'm a council member," he scoffs, as if that explains everything. Arrogant shit.

"Oh, so you want our people to fight while you do what exactly?" His face turns a slight shade of red. "Our people are peaceful beings." I'm addressing the entire room now, fully satisfied that Mr. Becker will shut his fucking mouth from now on. "I, for one, am proud to say our first instinct is *not* toward violence."

"How do we stop the government from hunting us down?" Mira, a respected council member, calls out.

"The vampire way," I declare. "Using intelligence instead of our fists. You wanted this," I boom. "So many in this room advocated for transparency. You wanted the humans to know, and now they do. I do not believe there is a single vampire here who thought revealing ourselves would go off without a hitch."

"Amelia is right," Mohan adds. "I have taken responsibility for my actions. I was hasty and delivered the news without thought. The president is acting out of instinct to an unknown threat."

"And if we try to resolve this using violence, we are giving her reaction validity. Humans have been fed lies about our kind for centuries. Of course, she wants to eradicate us. The woman is terrified. All humans with no prior knowledge of our existence will feel the same. So, we need to think as a group. Come up with a way to navigate this issue without bloodshed."

There is a wave of chatter. Erin enters my thoughts. Her presence soothes me. I briefly think of Erin's worry that these people will expect us to do something miraculous. I told her we didn't owe them an explanation. But in hindsight, they need to hear the truth. Erin and I cannot magically make this go away. We are humble vampires. Sure, we have new abilities, but they are the ones who have bestowed titles upon us and made us into something we are not.

"I know you expected Erin and I to come here with some grand plan. I'm sure many of you think we are the key to all vampire problems. We are not," I state. It's important to get that out there as soon as possible. "The Regina

Salvator has risen again. That is true. But that does not mean she is a God. Erin is a newly formed vampire. She is my mate. I am her protector, and together we are able to help our most vulnerable vampires. Humans too. But the buck stops there. We have elected leaders for a reason. No one vampire should have the fate of our kind resting on their shoulders."

"Here, here," Father calls. I send him a curt nod in thanks.

"For now, we must remain vigilant and hidden. If you have any ties that could be linked back to my family or Mohan, I strongly recommend that you do not go home yet."

Claire raises her hand. "What about our extended families?"

"If you feel they could be a target, do what you have to do to get them to safety. In the meantime, we need to brainstorm a way to get the president to step down her efforts to attack us."

Mohan clears his throat. "We need to concentrate on getting any families that need protecting into a safe house first. We will all think better once that is done."

"Yes," Erin says. "Nothing is more important than that. Council members, may I suggest you break off into your districts? We can formulate a plan after everyone is safe."

"Good thinking, Your Majesty," Mohan says, leaving me to roll my eyes again. I feel like a surly teenager again, close to straining my eyeballs. "You all know your constituents. Therefore, you are better suited to help them. However, if you need anything, do not hesitate to come forward. Is that agreeable to all?"

There are a few shouts of agreement, and all heads are nodding. It's not much, but it's a start. We can't even consider stopping the president if our minds are focused on the safety of our loved ones.

The crowd disperses, with every vampire jumping into action. I step off the chair and offer my hand to Erin. She gives me one of her smiles, one that, if we weren't surrounded by other people, would lead me to bend her over the closest bit of furniture. She sees my thoughts and bites her lips, quirking an eyebrow.

"I think that went well," Mohan whispers. Erin nods, as do I. "Would you both join me in the office for a moment?"

Gesturing with my hand, I step aside. "Lead the way."

As we enter the office, Mohan heads to a small bar and pours us all a glass of bourbon.

"Thank you for standing up there with me. It means a lot, especially after..." *You majorly fucked up?* Erin sends me a warning glare. Clearly, she doesn't want me voicing that particular thought.

"We need to be united," I say. "Surely, between us all we have enough places to hide any family members?"

"Yes, I believe so. Once that is done, the hard part begins," he says, swilling back the rest of his drink.

"Cheers to that." I chuckle because if I don't laugh, I'll probably cry.

"I'm exhausted." In fact, I could probably fall asleep standing up. Time moves strangely in the bunker. All the light is artificial and there isn't a clock in the main area, meaning all sense of time sort of vanishes.

"Sleep, my love. There isn't anything more to do today."

I wish it was that simple. Yes, I'm utterly spent, but my mind is struggling to shut off. There are so many things to think about. Organizing hideouts for the masses isn't easy.

There are so many moving pieces. If any of them fail, we could all be put in danger.

I've listened to dozens of stories from council members who recounted their own brush with the Secret Service or a military group. The president wasn't messing about; she wanted vampires dealt with swiftly. I still think she's an idiot for assuming we are so few. And for underestimating us. I presume she thinks we're just blood-thirsty savages, unable to string a sentence together without needing to drink from humans. Even though she's known Mohan for years, her basic instinct kicked in. How quickly she embraced old stories and myths.

"Amelia, you need to rest." Erin curls around me, her warmth easing my tense muscles.

"I can't relax. It's like a beehive in my head."

She chuckles. "Oh, I know."

Turning my head, I kiss her temple. "Sorry. I'll try to meditate."

She shifts beside me. "Or we could do something else."

Her voice is silky and full of heat. Ever since I let myself reconnect with her, our libidos are through the roof.

"Indeed. I think if you sat on my face, I would feel much better."

Her shoulders shake with silent laughter. "One face sitting, coming up," she jokes, but still moves her body over me.

Finally, my mind quiets as Erin's scent wraps itself around my olfactory senses. The fatigue I've battled with for the past few hours makes itself scarce. The thought of tasting my wife fills me with adrenaline, keeping me going for now, though I'm sure I'll collapse afterward.

"Patience," she teases. My hands are cupping her ass, trying to pull her pussy down to my salivating lips. Erin resists because she's naughty and loves to tease. Her hips dip slowly until I feel her wetness brush against my mouth. As I lift my head to lick her clean, she raises herself up and out of reach. "Someone's in a hurry."

"Erin," I growl. My fangs drop because I'm so wound up. I want to devour her.

"Put the teeth away and I'll let you have me." Her face is full of amusement.

Taking several deep breaths in through my nose and out through my mouth, I get myself under control and feel my teeth return to normal. "There, happy?"

Instead of retorting, Erin drops herself into my mouth. My hands redouble their efforts to bring her closer by grabbing her hips. She doesn't fight me this time. In fact, she grinds down hard. I love it when she rides my face.

Stripping off her own night gown—if that's what you can call a bit of silk that barely covers her body—Erin massages her breasts and pinches her nipples. Flinging her head back as she picks up speed, I am mesmerized by her beauty. Her golden hair falls behind her and brushes my knuckles as I hold on tight.

I'm definitely not the captain of this ship, but I couldn't care less. Erin's pleasure is running down my chin and her voice is getting louder as she commands my every move. My clit is aching by the time her scream fills the room.

No sooner has she finished do I feel her move off me. My legs fall open instantly, knowing I'm about to get what I need. Two fingers enter me roughly. Erin's body slides into place above me. Her mouth descends on me as she tastes herself. I can feel myself already close to the tipping point. Especially when she comments on how wet I am.

"Harder," I pant. Tonight I need it deep and fast. Reading my every thought, Erin plunges another finger inside until I am full. Her pace is relentless and after one particularly deep thrust, she curls her fingers, and I come undone. I couldn't tell you my name, let alone what I'd been worrying about. My mind is wonderfully clear as I float through our gold and blue auras. I'm sure the room lit up with our combined lights, but I didn't notice. I am lost in euphoria and Erin's eyes.

We lay silent for a while, allowing our breath to normalize.

"How are you feeling now?" Erin asks with a yawn, making me smile.

"I feel perfect. Sleep, my love."

Eight

ERIN

What a strange dream. It started off as any other. Amelia doing rather naughty things to me. But along the way, something changed. Amelia's talented fingers vanished, and I found myself transported elsewhere. It was almost like a Night Walk, but...not. Ugh, I can't describe it. I'm used to having the odd dream now and then, especially since my change. I should probably put it down to the enormous amount of stress Amelia and I have been under.

Speaking of my wonderful wife. I could have leaped across the room yesterday when she stepped up and held court. With all those vampires looking at me, I froze. The weight of everyone's future suddenly sat on my shoulders, and it was too heavy to hold. But, as usual, Amelia was my knight in black silk. Not only did she stand up and address the crowd of nervous families and council members, but she also looked fucking fantastic doing it. Which is why I was more than happy to help her relax in bed later. Hell, who am I kidding? I needed to feel her delectable tongue on me. My need for her has only gotten stronger over the years. Even when the timing is wildly inappropriate.

But then we fell asleep, and the dream happened. A mix between my reality and something else. Maybe *someone* else's. The sequence of events felt more like a string of memories, which I cannot quite get a grip on now as I lay here next to a slumbering Amelia.

I know there is more going on. I can feel the energy I usually expel on a Night Walk dancing across my skin, and if I'm not mistaken, I'm radiating a low golden glow. Yup, something weird went on in my sleep. But, as much as I would love to figure it out, there are more pressing matters at hand. For one, we will say goodbye to those who wish to leave the bunker and search for their friends and family today.

Second, we have to come up with some sort of plan to stop our kind from being targeted. Sounds simple, right? In all my newfound power, I'm useless at stopping the president. I've mulled over taking a walk into her subconscious, but a gut feeling tells me that would be a mistake. This is a delicate situation and needs finessing. As much as I would like to strong-arm her into seeing the error of her ways, I know I can't. Even if I could get through to her, we don't know who she has told. I'm sure there is a four-star general out there just champing at the bit to get his hands bloody. Amelia is right. Humans *do* love to kill what they don't understand.

Ugh, I'm driving myself nuts laying here ruminating. Coffee is required in the bucket loads. Turning over so my body is flush against Amelia, I take a second to watch her sleep. She's so beautiful. All the stress and anxiety washes from her face when she's in the land of dreams. I long for the lazy days spent in bed back at the penthouse. The endless hours we spent making love without a care in the world. Although I guess we never really had that. Our mating was fraught with the unknown from the very beginning.

Enough of that. I lean over and kiss her gently on the temple. She doesn't stir. Slipping out, I dress quickly and quietly before taking up my search for caffeine. The bunker is almost silent. I only know it's early morning because of the clock directly outside the bedroom. Underground living is not for me. I find it claustrophobic and detest the fact I can't feel the sun on my face. If we get through this, I'm going to need about six months of relaxation on a beach.

Lucille is the only person in the kitchen area. She looks like she hasn't slept at all. We silently catch each other's eyes in acknowledgment. Lucille is a shitty person in the morning, so God knows how cranky she'll be with little to zero sleep.

The coffee pot is full and begging for me to stick a straw in and drink directly from it. I'm not at home though, so I'll do the polite thing and pour a giant mug full. Settling down next to Lucille, I take several large gulps. My stomach is practically Teflon by now, so no worries about burning my mouth.

Lucille breaks the silence. "Amelia is still sleeping?"

"She's exhausted." That's an understatement.

Lucille nods. Her hand seizes mine, making me jump. Our eyes meet again, and I'm surprised to see unshed tears.

"I was so scared, Erin." The quiver in her voice is like a vise around my heart. Lucille is the strongest and most stoic out of the entire clan. To see her like this is hard to comprehend.

Taking her in my arms, I hold her tightly. "Me too," I whisper. What else can I say? I've spent the past two weeks terrified.

We stay like that for a minute until Lucille pulls back, wipes her face, and straightens her spine. "Don't tell assface about this, please."

"I'll take a wild stab in the dark and presume you mean Amelia?" I can't help but chuckle. These two will still bicker when we are a thousand years old, I swear it.

"You are correct." She grins. Her vulnerability stuffed back inside. "Do we know who intends to leave?"

I know she's changing the subject because she feels uncomfortable with the level of emotion she's just displayed, and that's fine.

"No one for sure. We will gather at nine a.m. to find out."

"What a clusterfuck." She sighs, shaking her head. "I used to admonish Amelia when she got on her high horse about humans. She was so sure they would be the end of us, and it looks like she was right."

"No, I wasn't." Amelia's sleep-soaked voice croaks from across the room. "I shouldn't have lumped an entire race in with a select few assholes." She strides over, leans down, and kisses me thoroughly. "Good morning, my love."

"Mmm," is all I can muster. Her kisses leave me speechless most days.

"Gross." Lucille mock gags.

"Morning to you, sister." Amelia grins, plastering a kiss on Lucille's cheek. I guess she overheard our discussion. "Have you finished crying?"

Yep, she definitely heard it.

Lucille's cheeks redden slightly before she reins it in. "Pft, I wasn't crying." She huffs. It's far too early for their shit.

Amelia. I almost growl internally.

She rolls her eyes at me and then winks. "I'm going to wake the family. I'd like some time together before we have to deal with anything else today. We've missed you all."

With that, Amelia leaves the room.

"Is Mohan a secret doomsdayer or something?" I ask as the Loch clan sits down to eat together. The family was more than happy to get up extra early to spend some time together.

"He bought the bunker off the family of a man who seemed to think Russia would be the end of the US," Harlan replies. "Mohan is a collector. That's why he has so many properties of varying shapes and sizes. However, he kept this one a secret, even from me."

My eyes scan the windowless walls. "So, it really is an end-of-days shelter. Interesting."

"It's a godsend," Victoria pipes up.

"It smells weird," Aliah comments, screwing up her nose.

"That's the scent of far too many vampires crammed into one place," Laurence supplies.

"After this is all over, maybe we can send out a national alert reminding people of the need to wash, or use deodorant," Lucas adds, grimacing. He's not wrong.

"Ah, my favorite vampires," Mohan calls entering the room. "Did you all sleep well?" He doesn't wait for an answer. "Sorry to interrupt, but there are a few people eager to get the meeting over with. Would you join us in the main hall?"

Without a word, we stop eating and rise from the table. I'm as keen as the rest of the family to know who will be leaving. I'm also excited to catch up with Claire, Kit, Jordan, Mack, and Chris.

The main hall is buzzing with people. Some have backpacks strapped to their bodies, clearly ready to leave. My heart plummets at the thought of them out there, far from the safety of the bunker. But they aren't my people to command. Amelia was right yesterday. Our roles are to help the Fallen and their mates. Not to rule.

"Can I have your attention, please?" Mohan calls. "For those who wish to leave, please come forward and put your name on the list."

Everyone shuffles from side to side as vampires snake through the crowd, trying to get to the list. My breath catches in my throat when I spot Mack and Jordan making their way over. Amelia has spotted them too, her eyebrows furrowed.

"Mack?" I call, snagging her attention. We embrace the second she is in reaching distance. Jordan hugs Amelia with force.

"It's so good to see you," Mack whispers into my neck. "We were so worried we'd not have time to see you before we left."

"Why the hell are you leaving?" Amelia asks, releasing Jordan and pulling Mack into her.

"We have friends in need, my Queen," Mack replies, bowing dramatically. Amelia bites her lip, her nostrils flaring. Mack loves nothing more than to wind her up. I suppress a laugh. Jordan doesn't.

"You're such a dick," Amelia grumbles. Mack laughs heartily.

"Where is Christopher?" I ask. The three are never far apart.

"He's collecting the rest of our things," Jordan says.

"Must you really go?" Emotion is sitting like a stone in my throat.

Mack takes my hand. "We do. You know there are still vampires out there who are vulnerable."

Mack, Jordan, and Chris have made it their mission to befriend as many nomadic vampires as possible. Most of them are people Amelia and I have helped. Even though they are mated, some of them spent a long time alone and haven't been able to integrate back into the community, preferring to wander the world with their beloved.

"What can we do?" Amelia asks. I know she would prefer to go along with them rather than stay here. Her protector is shining through, yearning to help.

"Come up with a way to stop the asshat we call our president from killing us all," Chris calls from behind. We turn and hug him.

"We'll do our best," I say. In truth, I'm scared our best won't be good enough.

"Where will you go?" Amelia asks.

Chris pulls out a map from his back pocket. We all shuffle over to the closest table. Laying the map out, I note several areas marked with red circles. "We will start on the West Coast and work our way across. Hopefully, we can reach all these marked spots."

Amelia scans the map. "Rendezvous points?"

Jordan nods. "We wanted a way to keep in touch with those who wished to continue wandering. You never know when you might need help, right?"

"Case and point," Mack adds, gesturing to our current surroundings.

"We set these locations as safe spots. We hope that any vampire that needs help will seek them out."

"We're relatively unknown," Jordan supplies. She's probably noticed my less-than-jovial demeanor. "Mack is the only one loosely linked to you, Erin. I don't think we will have a problem with anyone coming after us."

"It could still be dangerous," I add.

"We will be cautious. I promise," Mack replies.

"We have to help," Chris says, refolding the map. "Anyway, you can just do your mind thingy and see we're safe."

"*My mind thingy*." I laugh. "So technical."

"Eh, you know what I meant." He grins. "We'll be fine."

I hate it, but it's not my choice. My link to Jordan and Chris is still there. The bond we share makes their leaving harder than most.

"I'll check-in with you regularly. Please don't take any unnecessary risks. That goes for all of you."

With one last hug, I watch our friends sign the sheet and leave. My stomach is sour with worry. I thought that as soon as we reunited with the clan, we'd be okay. But it seems I was wrong. This shit is only just getting started and I've got to help bring it to a peaceful end.

But how?

Nine

AMELIA

I'm surprised by how many vampires have left the safety of the bunker. It was hard watching Mack, Jordan, and Chris go. Every part of me screamed to chase after them, to protect them. But my place is here, with Erin. Although, I'm not sure how long I can remain underground before I go insane. It's like the walls are closing in on me, squeezing the air from my lungs.

I feel the same energy radiating off Erin. We weren't meant to cower away and hide. This feels so wrong, but for the life of me, I don't know what else to do. A selfish part of me is happy that I have my family safe in this bubble of security under meters of concrete. That part of me doesn't want to do anything but curl up and wait for the storm to pass. Let someone else take the reins and figure it out. However, the bigger part of me, the warrior that rages inside, is itching to break free of these bare walls and seek our tormentor. Put an end to it once and for all.

Killing the President of the United States isn't something I thought I'd ever consider in my lifetime, but here we are. That small voice in my head whispers the merits of such actions. If she's gone, so is the threat. On the other hand, my guiding star, Erin, soothes me and makes me see reason. I wonder if my wife realizes how much I rely on her to keep me balanced, and not homicidal. I give a little chuckle at the thought. So much has changed over the past couple of years. Now I have to actively restrain myself from killing individuals who want to cause harm to my mate.

But the words I spoke to the vampires yesterday hold true. We have to find a peaceful end to this problem. I will not become a monster like the humans who hunt us. How tiring it is to have such warring thoughts constantly battling in my mind.

Erin's scent snaps me back to the here and now. She's across the room talking to Horatio. The family seems to have settled in. I guess they're just happy to be somewhere safe. Looking around, I see so many families, council members, and elders idly chatting, and then a feeling hits me low in my gut. We've been worrying so much about keeping everyone safe in here, we haven't spared a thought of how to keep the peace inside the bunker.

Eventually, the shock of being here will wear off and then we are left with a lot of people in the same space with nothing to do. That can only end in disaster. Idle hands and all that. I spot the little shit who opened his arrogant little mouth yesterday. He's lounging on a seat, barking orders at someone. I presume they must be on his staff. He's a prime example. It took him seconds to invite unrest into the group yesterday. What the hell will he be like in a few days?

I don't want to wait until we are on the brink of civil war down here until we address the problem. Feeling my concern, Erin looks over at me. I appreciate that she doesn't automatically read my mind. It's a boundary we feel is important. Although it doesn't always work and sometimes my emotions are too strong for her to ignore. Especially when I find it hard to express myself vocally.

I track her movements until she reaches me.

"What's wrong, honey?" she coos in my ear. Taking her hand, I pull her to our room. The last thing we need is for someone to overhear our conversations.

"We need to think of jobs for people to do. Having them lounge around without purpose is a bad idea, my love."

She studies my face before nodding. "You're right. We don't need boredom and frustration leading to problems."

"What about self-defense?" I say as the idea forms in my head. "I know we want to end this peacefully, but that doesn't mean they shouldn't be able to defend themselves if necessary," I say, flicking my head in the direction of the crowd. "The gym is big enough to start some training sessions."

"I like it. Maybe we could come up with other types of training sessions. Split them into smaller groups."

"Definitely. If they're occupied, it's less likely to end in disruption. Plus, they deserve to have a fighting chance. If for any reason we can't get the president to back down, I want to know our people can fend for themselves."

"Let's talk to Mohan and get something set up. The sooner the better."

We head out of the bedroom and search for the Grand Master. My anger toward him is at a palatable level now. I think I will always harbor some resentment because my warrior demands it. But I can move on now.

Mohan is more than happy to do whatever we suggest. I think he's just grateful not to be dealing with this alone. Now we have to put it to the people. I have a feeling that some, especially council members, will balk at the idea of doing anything. Complacency is ripe within the rich and entitled. Huh, maybe we're not so different from humans after all.

Honing years of getting attention from an unruly Loch clan, I stick two fingers in my mouth and create an ear-piercing whistle. Everyone falls silent and turns to me.

"Thank you," I begin. "Erin and I would like to put something to you, if you'd be so inclined to give me a few moments of your time."

A few vampires settle into chairs while others lean against the nearest bit of furniture, ready to listen. I wait a few more moments, allowing stragglers to settle down. The bunker really is massive.

"Erin and I would like to offer training sessions." No need to bullshit them. "Self-defense being one."

"Oh, so you want us to fight now?"

Ah, Mr. Becker, the little asshole strikes again.

"We want you to be able to defend yourself. That's vastly different from seeking out a fight, Mr. Becker."

"We would also like to train you in other things, such as survival and communications," Erin says. I'm guessing she's just made that up on the fly. "There are plenty of you who have experienced war."

"We're at war now, too," Mr. Becker sneers, and my warrior finally loses her shit. In a blur, I move to him, my rather impressive and terrifying fangs bared. I see the color drain from his face as I tower over him.

"Do you have anything else to add?" I growl. "If so, speak now."

I'm not going to hurt him. I don't feel out of control, but I do want him to shut his fucking mouth, and if I have to intimidate the little prick to get that result, I'm okay with it. He swallows thickly, his eyes dancing between my eyes and fangs. There aren't many people who have seen me like this. He shakes his head and speaks, but it is so low, even I barely hear it.

"Say again, Mr. Becker. I didn't quite get that."

"N-no. I-I have nothing more to add."

I lean even closer until my lips are by his ear. "If you cause a problem down here, Mr. Becker, we will be having another chat, and next time, I won't be so calm. Understood?"

Once again, he nods, but this time remains silent. I stand to my full height and purposefully keep my fangs in full view. Turning on the spot, I let the crowd see me.

"Let me be clear," I say confidently. "We are not going to war, but our lives have changed. Learning how to defend yourself and your family is the most basic thing we can offer you. Knowing how to survive out there should the worst happen is invaluable to you, but neither Erin nor I will force you to learn. However, I will not tolerate individuals causing trouble. We have enough strife to contend with, without unrest being cultivated in here. If you have something to get off your chest, come to me, Erin, or Mohan."

"Amelia is right," Mohan says, stepping to my side. "These are trying times ahead. Bickering amongst ourselves will do no good. I urge you to learn basic skills. We are strong together. We can get through this, but we have to work as one. As we always have."

"I offer myself as an instructor," Lucille says from behind me. "I'm an accomplished martial arts fighter. I'm happy to teach anyone willing to learn."

"I can teach map reading," Marcus calls.

"We went through two World Wars as spies," my mother adds. "Happy to pass on some tricks of the trade."

"You were spies?" Erin asks. "That's so cool."

The tension in the room breaks with several vampires chuckling at my wife's awed face and outburst.

"What do you all say?" I ask, making eye contact with as many people as possible.

Paula steps forward. "I'd love to learn how to read maps, and Ricco would like to help pass on some of his Ranger training. Sign us up."

And just like that, the tide turns. Instead of fear sitting in the air, excitement crackles. People have smiles across their faces, and their body language loosens.

You can put them away now, honey.

I turn to look at Erin, who is biting her bottom lip. Her gaze is firmly on my mouth. The little minx is turned on. She has a thing for my teeth. I grin and lick the tip of my left fang. Her eyes go remarkably black.

Lucille punches me in the arm. "Can you keep it in your panties? We've got people to train." A low growl rumbles in my throat. "Oh, calm down. You can fuck her later. After we've organized this lot."

Erin stands with her hand covering her mouth. I can see her shoulders shaking.

Later, my love.

And then she winks and turns away.

Great, now I'm frustrated and horny. I need to expel some energy. Spotting Mr. Becker trying to slink off, I take several steps toward him.

"Are you interested in self-defense?" I ask.

He jumps at the sound of my voice. "I've never given it much thought," he replies unsteadily.

"Spar with me." I don't know why I'm doing this. The man is awful, but he still deserves to have the opportunity. "You're arrogant, Mr. Becker. And entitled. I've seen the way you speak to people." His face grows red. "Tell me this. In the event of an emergency, who would come to your aid?"

"I..."

"I would. I would help you because you are a part of my community. Can you say you'd do the same?"

"I..."

"Don't be that person, Mr. Becker. Be better than the people we are up against. Be a part of this community. Help people less fortunate than yourself. As you stated previously, you are a council member. Act like one."

We are silent for several moments before he straightens. "I apologize, Mrs. Loch, for my outbursts. It appears I do not handle stress too well. I *am* better than this."

"Then spar with me. Let me teach you. Then take what you've learned and help others."

"I would be honored," he says, bowing slightly. I could've done without that, but whatever.

I feel as if I have control over something at last. I spend the next several hours organizing our impromptu training sessions. I also spend time beating the crap out of Lucille for "demonstration" purposes. By the time we finish, both Lucille and I have grins plastered on our faces.

The bunker is a hive of positivity and focus. My family is at the forefront of it, which makes my chest ache with pride. I spot Mr. Becker with several others, including Ricco, as they walk through some defensive steps. He's taken off his suit jacket and rolled up his sleeves. I even see him laugh along with the woman he was directing earlier.

We haven't come up with a plan yet, but this is definitely progress.

Ten

ERIN

Seven days. Seven whole, long days we have been in the bunker, and I can feel my skin getting paler by the second. You'd think for vampires it wouldn't be a big deal. But as you know, contrary to the tales, vampires do not look like sickly Victorians with dysentery. If I close my eyes and concentrate, I can feel the sun's warmth on my face. Hear the sea crashing against the rocks. It's like I'm there, standing on the beach Amelia took me to on one of our first dates. I miss my tan and the smell of fresh air, which is a super selfish thing to think about while we're going through a crisis, but that's where my mind is today.

Speaking of crisis, Amelia really helped divert us from one by suggesting we keep the masses occupied. In fact, it's done wonders for everyone involved. Amelia in particular. For me, though, it has only left me with crushing anxiety that I have been masking from my wife. You see, while the families and council members do their utmost to learn new skills, I've been racking my brain, trying desperately to come up with a plan to end this without bloodshed. The result? Nada. Zilch. Zero. And on top of that, I'm having these weird dreams every night.

There is a feeling in my chest that is telling me the dreams are important. That I should take detailed notes of everything I see. The problem is, by the time I come to recount them, the images have slipped through my fingers like sand.

Before I trouble Amelia with it, I'm going to find Barty. As far as we know, he is the oldest living vampire. Maybe he can help me decipher their meaning, or at least the feeling I have of the dream's relevance to our current situation.

Anya and Barty have been spending a lot of time in and out of the bunker. Barty has a lot of contacts, more than Mohan, and they are turning out to be invaluable. We can get real-time reports on the president and her efforts toward finding us. The woman doesn't realize she has the "enemy" literally by her side on a daily basis. I can't even imagine what it is like for the vampires close to the country's leader, knowing what she wants to do to our kind.

Barty and Anya returned last night, so before they head out again, I'm going to track them down and have a chat. However, that's easier said than done in this place. Every time I move, someone wants to talk to me, thank me, bow to me, or, in one painful instance, drop to their knees and begin praying at my feet. I found myself emulating Amelia by rolling my eyes. How quickly people jump on the worship bandwagon. I might be the Salvator Regina reincarnated or whatever, but I'm no goddess. Unless you listen to Amelia when I do a certain thing with a certain object close to a certain orifice. Anyway, that's not the point. I'm lucky to have the power to help the Fallen, but that doesn't mean I should be seen as a deity.

Okay, that's all for my daily gripe. I need to focus and find Barty as quickly as possible. Fortunately, the universe seems to give me a break. I almost plow into Anya as soon as I leave the bedroom. She looks great as usual. No one would know she's been on clandestine trips, which put her and her mate's life in danger. I hope I look that calm, collected, and cute.

"Just the person, or one of them, I was looking for."

Anya smiles and tugs me into her body. "Erin, you're looking good. How are you?"

"In need of you and Barty's counsel, if possible?"

"Of course. Come on."

I link my arm in Anya's as we walk. She fills me in on their latest trip outside. Barty wanted to meet up with a contact who works in the Senate. As far as we know, the president is still keeping the existence of vampires close to her chest. That buys us some time. I shudder to think what would happen if she made the news public. Maybe she's worried that the country would think she's nuts.

Barty is lounging on a couch in their room with a large whisky. As usual, he's wearing a golf sweater and pants. I almost feel bad for interrupting his downtime. I'm sure he and Anya want nothing more than to spend some quality time together. They've lived in near seclusion in their Irish castle for so long, I wonder if being around so many vampires is difficult.

"Erin, love, how are ya?" Barty's smile is wide and genuine.

"Hey Barty," I say softly, giving him a hug. "As good as can be. I hear your trip was positive."

"Aye, well, at least we don't have to worry about the US Army coming after us. Not yet."

"The Special Forces are the US Army," I say.

"Special being the operative word. They are top security, meaning the president isn't ready to broadcast it to the world we exist. Plus, there are only so many Special Forces soldiers. Easier to deal with than a battalion, right?"

"True. Silver linings, I suppose."

"Where's Amelia?" Anya asks, handing me a glass of wine.

I chuckle. "Probably beating the crap out of Lucille. I've truly never seen her so happy."

We share a laugh. In truth though, Amelia has stepped up and is in her element helping to train anyone who wishes to learn self-defense. I see a permanent blue shimmer across her skin as her warrior rejoices in the work she is doing.

"Lucille is a firecracker." Barty raises his eyebrows. "She near on put me through the wall when I had a training session with her."

"Oh poor baby," Anya soothes, kissing him on his head. "You forget you're an old man now, dear."

"Pft, I'm as fit as a fiddle. Just not as fit as the Loch girls."

"Few people are," I comment with a grin. My mind pictures Amelia's strong body. "I think Amelia and Lucille have made it into a competition to see who is the strongest. From what I know, Lucille has always had the upper hand until Amelia changed."

"Well, it will be a while until I get back in the ring with either of them." We sip our drinks. "Something tells me you didn't find me to have a chat about Amelia's fighting skills or the competition with her sister."

"Nope." I sigh. "I've been having strange dreams."

"Dreams?" Anya repeats.

"Yes...well, maybe they are more than dreams. I feel like I'm Night Walking, but...not. I can't put my finger on it. Since we've been in the bunker, they have become frequent. By the time I wake up, I can't grasp what I saw."

Barty scratches his chin. "And you think they are relevant?"

I shrug my shoulders. "That's the problem. I don't know."

"But you have a feeling?" Anya asks.

Nodding, I run my hand through my hair. It needs a trim. "Something in me says yes. They are important."

"We shouldn't rule anything out, especially where you're concerned, Erin. Your abilities are unique. The dreams could be a new development."

"Like what? I've... Hang on, I know what they feel like." God, why didn't I think of it sooner? "The time I connected with Amelia and she allowed me to live her past through her eyes. It was more than being present in her mind. It was as if we became one. Very intense."

I've witnessed Amelia's memories several times over the years, but that particular moment was different. We'd made love for hours, and our bond had never felt stronger. I felt our life forces become one entity that day.

Barty gets up from the couch and heads to a desk piled high with paper. He spends a few minutes searching until he holds up a folder. "This is everything I have on the original Salvator Regina. Maybe the answer is in here."

I spent the afternoon pouring through the file Barty handed me. There wasn't anything in there that gave me solid answers. What I need is a way to record my dreams.

Or at least remember enough to give me an inkling of what their significance is.

We eat with the family in one of the dining rooms. I make an effort to engage in the conversations happening around me, but my mind is preoccupied. A spark of an idea is slowly igniting in the back of my mind. It's true that the time Amelia allowed me to see her life was extremely intimate. What if we can recreate that but in reverse? Could I attach my subconscious to Amelia, joining us as one while I sleep? Would she be able to see what I see?

"Are you alright, my love?" Amelia whispers in my ear.

I turn my head and bring the present into focus. "We need to talk after dinner."

Her eyes search mine. "Okay. We can leave now if you want?"

I find myself nodding. I'd usually wait until the night came to an organic end, but frankly, I just can't think of anything else right now.

After politely excusing ourselves and giving cheek kisses to everyone, we retire to our room. Amelia occupies herself while I change into sweatpants and a t-shirt.

"Sit with me," I finally say.

Over the next twenty minutes, I explain what's going on with me and the subsequent discussion I had with Barty and Anya. Amelia remains silent for a few moments once I've finished talking. I see the hurt in her eyes. She's upset I didn't tell her about the dreams as soon as they started happening.

"Since when do we keep things from each other?"

"Honey," I begin. "It's not like that. We've just had other things going on and I didn't want to add one more unanswerable thing to our plate."

"But it is like that. You've been actively shielding yourself from me."

I cock my eyebrow. "I know what that feels like."

Scrubbing her hands over her face, she grins. "Touché. But I don't like that this is something we are doing to each other. I know we put some boundaries in about reading each other's minds, and I still think they are a good idea. But not this. Not hiding important things from each other. Are *we* okay? Should I be worried?"

"Hey, hey. Slow down. We have nothing to worry about. Not about us. We are a part of each other. I think it's natural to want to keep troubling and potentially painful things from the person you love more than life itself."

"I guess. But I think we need to stop. I want you to come to me about these things. I'm your mate, Erin."

"As you are mine. I promise not to keep things from you again."

She kisses me with passion. "I promise too. Now, about this idea. Do you really think we can link like that?"

"I honestly don't know, but I don't have any other ideas."

"The issue is, you'll be unconscious. How can we keep tethered?"

"My theory. And it really is just a theory, is that when we become one. When you are me, you'll have the power to control the link. It's not a simple Night Walking. We are merging. Just like we did when I saw your past."

"Okay. What do we have to lose? I think we should have Barty and Anya here when we do it."

"Kinky." I grin.

Amelia rolls her eyes. "I don't share," she growls playfully.

"Oh, I know," I murmur, licking the side of her neck.

"Erin, focus." She chuckles. "If something goes wrong, one of them can wake us up."

"That could be dangerous."

"So could getting permanently stuck in your mind."

"Hmm, you're right. It is a filthy place." I purr. Okay, I just can't stop myself when I'm around her.

"Clearly, I need to make you come a few times before we do this. I can't have you acting like a horny teenager when I'm bonding with your conscience."

My smile is as wide as the Cheshire cat. "I think you do, too. At least three, I think."

Amelia licks her lips. "On all fours, Erin. Ass up."

Eleven

AMELIA

After thoroughly debauching Erin, I should be on a high. But as is the normal now, my mind is firmly on other things. Namely, this dream connection idea. I don't know what else to call it.

A small part of me is still agitated that Erin kept it from me, but that would make me a massive hypocrite after I kept my anxieties regarding my warrior to myself for so long. Still, it begs the question. Should I be worried about my marriage? Erin doesn't think so, and surely I'm overreacting. After all, she is the other half of my soul. But that doesn't mean that we won't have speed bumps as a couple. I'm no expert, but keeping secrets from each other can't be good. We're still fledglings in the grand scheme of things. Erin and I will have thousands of years together. We can't be failing already. Right?

Erin is unconscious and I intend to keep her that way, at least until I have found Barty. I think having him in the room as we attempt this connection is wise. I have no idea if he'll be able to actually help if, God forbid, anything goes sideways. But his presence is a comfort nonetheless.

Before Barty, I think a visit with my parents is in order. They have a solid two hundred years of marriage between them. If they can't advise me, who can? Hopefully they will tell me I'm overreacting, and my marriage is not on the rocks.

My parents are chatting cordially with a few council members. The night is still young, according to the clock outside our room. Hopefully, they won't mind me stealing them away from their nightly martini.

"Good evening, everyone," I say to the group. My mother gives me a beaming smile, but I can see the questions already forming in her eyes.

"Amelia, I thought you'd retired for the evening, dear."

"Not quite. Could I steal you and Father away for a moment?"

"Of course. Please excuse us," she says to the group.

Mother and Father follow me as I make my way to Mohan's office. Thankfully, he isn't in it. I close the door behind us. "What's wrong?" Mother instantly asks.

"Nothing to be alarmed about, I assure you. Drink?" Mohan has an impressive collection of spirits in here. I set about pouring three martinis. No reason their routine should be interrupted.

"Thank you, sweetheart," Father says. "Are you sure you're okay?"

I sit opposite them on a plush single-seat armchair. "I'm a little worried about Erin and I."

That earns an eyebrow raise from both parents.

"In what way?" Mother asks, her drink forgotten about.

Taking a deep breath, I fill them in on the things Erin and I have been keeping from each other, including the dreams and our plan.

"We're still so new at this. Erin is my entire universe. She's my soulmate, and I'm hers. So why are we keeping such important things from each other?"

"Have you spoken to Erin about this?" Father asks.

"Yes, earlier on. She doesn't feel we have a problem."

"But that hasn't convinced you?" Mother replies.

"It's not about convincing me. I'm terrified of screwing this up." And there is the reality of it. Our world has been chaotic for so long, I barely feel I'm holding on. What happens if I can't keep a grip on my marriage either? If I lost Erin, I would cease to exist. There has never been an instance of a mated couple separating. But then again, there has never been a couple like me and Erin. We seem to break new ground in many ways, and I can't stand to think that we could be the first mated vampire couple to fall apart.

Father puts his drink on the table. "Amelia, my sweet, disregard the fact that you are mated. Your souls bonded. A blind man could see the love Erin has for you. She is utterly immersed in you, as you are her."

"Your father is right. And who says other couples don't have problems? We are still individuals, still have differences. Your father slept on the couch for weeks after Laurence was born."

"Really, why?"

"I fell short in helping your mother with our newborn son and rightfully, she got angry."

"We've had some whopper arguments over the years, Amelia. We've also kept things from each other. We know what it's like to have your other half able to read thoughts, remember? In my opinion that puts an extra strain on the relationship at times. It is natural to guard some thoughts, especially if you think they may upset your other half."

"Your mother's right. Marriage can be hard work at times, regardless of how much you love each other. And I think you need to remember what you've both been through to get where you are."

"You've always guarded your heart, Amelia. It will take time for old habits to die. Just keep talking to one another and everything will be fine."

I blow out a breath. "Thank you, and I'm sorry. I feel silly now."

"Nonsense. We all still need our parents from time to time, no matter how old we are."

"Grandfather and Grandmother will be so pleased to hear that," I quip.

My mother laughs. "I'm sure. When they return from wherever they are, I'll be sure to tell them."

We all laugh. My grandparents on both sides are perpetual wanderers. It's been at least fifteen years since I saw any of them. The last I heard, they were somewhere in the Arctic. Northernmost Alaska, I think. Unlike my parents, none of them ever enjoyed politics. They never wanted to be involved in the community beyond the occasional dinner party. I envy them to some degree. I'm not surprised one jot that they've no clue what's going on. If they did, they'd be here. Maybe word will reach them eventually. In all honesty, the longer they stay out of it, the better. I want them to enjoy their solitude. Maybe when this is over, I can track them down. Erin would love ice fishing. We could snuggle up in an igloo and forget the world.

My father shuffles forward and places a hand on my knee. "You're doing a fine job, Amelia. Trust Erin when she tells you it's all okay."

I nod. "I will." Squeezing their hands, I stand. "Now I've kept you long enough. I need to find Barty."

We hug.

"Be careful," Mother whispers in my ear.

I still feel a little silly for needing my parents' reassurance that I'm not fucking up my marriage. I'm going to need some serious therapy when this is all over.

I try my best to push all that to the back of my mind as I make my way to Barty and Anya's quarters. Anya answers the door in a rather revealing negligée. Her hair is tousled, and she has a certain glow on her cheeks. I'm glad they're getting some quality time together. Although I'm about to rain all over it.

"Evening," I smirk. "Sorry to interrupt."

"I wouldn't have answered the door if that were the case," Anya winks. "Barty's in the shower."

"Can I come in for a second?"

Anya steps aside and lets me in. The air is thick with sex. My mind rushes back to Erin and to the filthy things I did to her earlier on. A shiver slips up my spine.

Anya's giggle brings me back to reality. "Looks like I'm not the only one who's had a good night so far."

I grin. "Erin told you about the dreams." It's not a question. "We need your help again."

Barty steps out of the bathroom in just a towel. If I had any inclination toward the male sex, I'd be impressed. "What do you need?"

"For you to put some clothes on before your wife jumps you again." I laugh. Anya looks like she wants to devour him. Barty laughs. Once he is dressed, and Anya is no longer salivating, I tell them the plan.

Barty rubs his chin in contemplation. "It's worth a shot. I'm out of my depth really, Amelia, but if Erin thinks it will work, we're happy to stand guard. Are we attempting it this evening?"

I nod. "Could you come over in, say, half an hour?"

Erin is no longer asleep by the time I slip back into our room. She eyes me with concern. "I really don't enjoy waking up to find you gone, honey."

Striding over, I sit on the bed and take her face in my palms. I kiss her deeply until we are both breathless.

"Forgive me," I murmur into her mouth.

"Always," she whispers. "Where did you go?"

"To find Barty. He and Anya will be over shortly. And..."

"And?"

I exhale slowly. "I spoke to my parents. About us. I got in my head about our secret keeping."

"I knew it," she replies, brushing her nose against mine. "Did they help?"

"Yes. I'm sorry, my love. Sometimes I feel like a teenager trying to navigate an adult's life. I'll do better. I want to be the perfect wife for you."

"Neither of us will be perfect, honey. We are fine, though. I promise you."

"I know. Sometimes I just need reassuring," I say, taking her lips again.

Before we get lost in each other's bodies again. There is a knock at the door. It's amazing how fast time slips by when you're having fun. Or about to.

Everyone exchanges the usual pleasantries. I think we're all ready to get this over and done with.

"I'll connect with Amelia's mind while awake. Hopefully, I will be able to slip into sleep after," Erin says, making herself comfortable on the bed.

"Should I try to sleep too, or stay awake?"

"It could be the connection forces you into the same state as me. Try to stay conscious, and just go with whatever comes along." Erin is so calm, whereas I have alarm bells ringing through my body. "Barty, Anya, if we seem in distress, attempt to wake me gently."

"Will do," Barty confirms.

Erin takes my hand. "Ready?"

No. "Ready."

We lay side by side, but that isn't going to work for me. I need Erin in my arms. Pulling her close, she curls around my body easily. Her hand rests on my cheek as her head lies on my chest. My heart is beating wildly.

Relax, my love.

Tapping into every meditation technique I know, I force my heart and mind to relax. The key to our connection is to open our minds completely. It takes mere seconds for Erin to make her presence known. We've done this countless times now, but the next part will be harder. Well, for Erin. She's the one who has to forge the connection with me and flip it, so I become one with her mind.

Turning my head slightly, I rest my nose in her hair. Her scent invades me until I feel consumed with her. A gold mist creeps into my mind's eye as I concentrate on Erin's smell. I close my eyes and let her in. My warrior invites her with open arms, almost giddy to embrace the golden light.

I know it has worked. It's just a feeling. I can't explain how. I am her, and she is me. Now we must wait and see if I can control the connection. Erin's mind becomes foggy as she slips into sleep. Concentrating with all that I have, I let the fog surround me, but not overpower me. Through it, I feel the tendrils of Erin's connection. My mind plucks at them. They vibrate as they surrender to my will.

I have control.

The fog recedes but the golden threads remain wrapped in my hands. A scene unfolds in front of me. It's hazy at first but becomes crystal clear quickly. Erin is right. This is no simple dream. I can feel the power of it already.

A vast jungle spreads out before me. The sound of birds is almost overwhelming. The smell of fire snags my attention. My feet move and I am powerless to stop them.

The vines seemingly move out of my way by themselves. I'm almost gliding now. The smell of burning gets stronger. Movement up ahead has me straining to get there faster, but I can't. My grip on our connection is waning. The scene is blurring. I just need a little longer, and I know I will find the answers we've been looking for. I engage my warrior to help me forge on, but as I break through to a clearing, my mind goes black.

My body bolts upright from the bed as I struggle to inhale. Anya is by my side in an instant. I turn to make sure Erin is okay. Her eyes are open. She smiles.

"It worked," she says. "And we need to do it again."

Twelve

ERIN

It worked! It really worked. Not only were we able to connect, but Amelia could see everything I saw and control it. And the best part is that I can remember the dream. All of it. The lush jungle, the potent smell of wood burning. The birds. Oh, my god, they were so loud. If I close my eyes again, I swear I can feel the wind against my cheek as it blew through the canopy of trees. There was something, or someone. We were so close to seeing them, but I couldn't hold on. The combined effort of linking to Amelia and exploring the dream world was exhausting.

Amelia knows the dream is important. We both felt it the moment we saw our surroundings. Now, we just have to figure out what it means. That spark in my chest is now a raging inferno. Whatever we saw is the key to our current problem. I'm sure of it, but don't ask me how I know because I have no fucking clue.

"We need to do it again," I say, full of confidence. If we could just reach the spot where the noise was coming from, I know we will have what we need to figure it out.

"Not tonight, my love. You look as exhausted as I feel," Amelia replies. I want to argue but my body feels like lead.

"What did you see?" Barty asks. I almost forgot they were here.

"We were in the jungle," Amelia begins. "That was no dream. It was like we were being guided."

I nod. "Yes. I'd put money on that being an actual place in the world."

"So, something or someone is leading you?" Anya asks.

"Yes," I state. "We should try again as soon as we are rested."

Amelia falls asleep moments after Barty and Anya leave. It's late and I know I should follow her lead, but my mind is whirring with questions. First and foremost, what does this mean? I thought I had finished my change. Am

I developing another kind of power? Will I keep evolving? The thought sends a shiver down my spine. I think I've dealt with everything pretty well so far, but the unknown is scary. I still want to resemble Erin Hanson-Loch when all is said and done. If parts of me keep changing, I'm not sure who I'll be.

My mind wanders back to my old life. The days when my only worries were making enough money to pay rent and sifting through potential women to date. A small part of me longs for those simple times. But then I think of my life without Amelia Loch in it and I feel sick. I know I'd give up my mortal life a million times over and fight the entire world to be with her.

Then I wonder what our life would have been like if Amelia met me as a human herself. Without the pull of her soul reaching for mine, would she still have been attracted to me? I like to think so. Even though Dr. Mendhi was an awful person, I believe his theory about vampires having free will is true. I think Amelia had to choose me as much as I did her. Our attraction goes beyond a predetermined bond. Amelia would have captured my heart, regardless.

I like to fantasize about what our life would look like if we were both human. Would we have met in Insomnia?

Would Amelia still be the powerhouse who owns upscale bars and clubs, or would she be a totally different person?

If she were the boss of Insomnia still, I'm sure she would have pissed me off just the same by coming behind the bar and taking a drink out of the fridge. She would have charmed me with her wit and sultry eyes and I'm guessing I would have ended up in her bed a lot faster than I did in reality.

Truthfully, I wouldn't change our life for the world. We just need to get through this, and everything will calm down. We are due for some peace and tranquility. That's why it's imperative I figure out the message being delivered to me through these dreams.

I'm about to do something that my wife is going to be very upset about. I'm going to hijack her mind as she sleeps. I know how to link us and flip the connection now. If I'm right, Amelia will slip from whatever dream world she's currently in to mine once I'm asleep. The moment she's connected, she'll know what I've done, and I'm sure she will have plenty to say, but I can't wait another minute. I have to see to understand.

Taking her hand, I give her a silent apology before delving into her mind. She's dreaming of rather adult activities which makes me smile. I love that even in sleep she can't get enough of us.

I forge the bond quickly and settle into the bed, ready for sleep myself. I can already feel her confusion bubbling up as she feels the conversion from X-rated fun to something else. With no time to waste, I meld our consciousnesses together until she is me, and then I settle my mind, allowing sleep to claim me. Irritation prickles my skin as Amelia makes her thoughts known.

Our jungle world snaps into view with a stark contrast. It seems brighter this time around. The birds are just as loud, and the smell of fire still permeates the air. We turn toward a sound. I utilize Amelia's superior hearing to listen. The wind gently blows and that's when I hear it. A whisper in the air, calling me.

Erin.

That's it, just my name.

Willing my legs to move, I could cry in relief when I suddenly float toward the trees where I know our answer is waiting for us. This time, I don't have the weight of exhaustion pulling me back to reality. It's like my subconscious knows I must hold on. My hand reaches out before me to sweep away a curtain of vines, and then I see it. A simple hut in a clearing. There is no one around, but the fire burns. A pot hangs over it, presumably cooking the occupant's meal. My eyes scan feverishly, hoping to meet whomever it is that is calling me to them. Nothing. I want to scream in frustration.

Amelia sends a wave of calm over us, tempering my rising fire. Taking a slow, deep breath, I refocus. If I can't find the person, maybe I can find clues as to where we are. I'm convinced more than ever that this is a place in the world hidden in the trees. Hidden from society. As the thoughts enter my mind, I see blue and gold hues encircle the hut. There is no clearer sign than mine and Amelia's auras are involved.

In the distance, I can see a distinctly jagged rock formation. It rises like shards of glass sticking up from the earth. I can use that. I just hope I'm able to remember them when I wake up. I take in every edge, every tree sticking up from the landscape, and burn them into my mind.

The tug of our failing connection tells me we only have seconds before the jungle will disappear and I'm certain that Amelia won't be in the mood to visit again anytime soon. She's really mad at me.

I know Amelia is glaring at me before I open my eyes, and I doubt I can use my womanly charms to get out of trouble this time. Peeking one eyelid open, I try for the look-how-cute-I-am-and-how-adorable-you-find-my-rule-breaking. It does not work. Her eyes turn into black holes and her fangs descend. Her inner warrior is making her displeasure known, too.

"Are you serious, Erin? You kidnapped me in my sleep?"

Heat creeps up my throat. "That's a bit much, honey. I just brought you along for the ride!"

She growls at me. "A ride we weren't supposed to go on until we were both rested and willing, Erin!"

I sit up and shuffle to her side. "Okay, I know I shouldn't have done that. I'm sorry."

Her eyebrow raises. "No, you're not."

"Ugh, fine. I'm not sorry because we got what we needed, Amelia." How can she not see the logic in my decision?

"We could have got nothing and ended up in trouble, Erin. And that's bypassing the fact you not only disregarded our boundaries, but you also obliterated them."

Okay, she might have a point. I did cross a line in pursuit of answers. This, off the back of our recent secret-keeping saga, doesn't look good.

Pulling myself even closer, I nuzzle my nose into her neck. "I am sorry for that, my love. I'll never do it again, I swear."

"Consent, Erin. That's all I'll say."

My heart drops to my stomach. She's completely right. I didn't just take her for a ride-along. I violated her privacy. Jesus, why did I do that? Maybe I'm the one that should be worried about turning into a monster. Nothing is worth taking someone's choice away from them. My god, I feel sick. It's one thing soothing her mind when she has nightmares. It's quite the other taking control away from her.

"Whoa, okay, clam down." Amelia is wrapping her arms around me.

A stuttered breath heaves out. "I-I'm sorry honey, I wasn't thinking clearly. I just wanted the answer so badly. I shouldn't have done that." My voice turns into a sob.

"It's okay. Please don't cry."

"It's not okay," I rasp. "It's not okay at all."

She rocks me back and forth silently as I cry. Along the way, I've forgotten what it means to have the ability to walk through other people's minds and the responsibility that puts on my shoulders. I would be devastated if someone traipsed through my thoughts without consent. No matter what adversity we are facing, I can never forget that.

After several more minutes, I lean back and kiss her. She looks at me with her usual adoration and it makes me feel even more guilty. That's something I'll have to live with, I guess.

"Did you see the rocks in the distance?" she says, changing the subject. "We should be able to use them to identify where in the world they are."

I swallow and urge myself to move on, even though I don't deserve her forgiveness so easily. "Yes, I saw them. Did you hear the wind?"

"Calling your name. Yes. We're definitely onto something. I suggest we enlist Marcus. He seems to have a knack for maps and research."

"Before we do that... Will you just hold me for a while?" I feel awful and vulnerable, and the only person who can comfort me is the same person I hurt.

"I'll hold you forever, you know that."

I wish she could. I wish we were anywhere but here, in this situation.

Thirteen

AMELIA

I t's the first time I have been truly angry with Erin. However, the second I saw her devastation, I had to let it go. She will carry that with her for a long time to come. There's no reason for me to pile on. Not when we have important work to get done. Finding the location of that hut being at the top of the list.

After I've held her for an hour, we shower separately and dress quickly. Marcus is our first port of call. He's proven himself to be quite the bookworm, and I'm positive he will be the key to finding that hut.

We make our way to the common room. People have already gathered in groups to discuss their upcoming day.

I'm so pleased the training sessions are such a success. One last thing to worry about. The most surprising has to be Mr. Becker. The arrogant little shit that called out during that first day here is nowhere to be seen. He's buckled down and has become one of the hardest-working vampires in the bunker.

The rest of the family is already at the table. We seem to have claimed it as our own. Well, in fairness, we are the largest family in here, number wise, I mean.

"Good morning, my loves," Mother calls. I take my time walking around the table and kissing everyone hello. Even Lucille.

"Morning everyone. Are we all well rested?" My question is answered by several affirmations. Erin gives a small smile but says nothing. I know Mother will spot her mood in an instant.

"Mohan has decided to send a group out to gather some supplies. We need a fresh stock of Red," my father says.

"Makes sense. Who is he sending?"

"Me," Lucille says. "Considering I'm the fastest here."

I scoff. "Not by a mile, dear sister. You've yet to see me at full speed. Actually, you wouldn't see me. That's the point. I'm afraid you'll be taking second place from now on."

It feels normal and fun to poke Lucille. She's always up for a bit of a scrap.

"You know, I won't even argue. You are faster." She laughs at my disappointed pout. "Sorry to rain on your parade."

"How about we spar later?"

"Deal." She winks. "I'll find you when I'm back. I'm taking Mr. Becker. He's turning out to be quite skilled."

"You're not teaching him to fight, I hope?"

Lucille rolls her eyes. "No, I'm not. But Mr. Becker is an exceptional student and I'm happy to train him in martial arts. I don't believe he has nefarious reasons, Amelia. I think the distraction from all this is the driving force."

I nod. "Fine. Be safe out there." She nods in return.

"Would you all excuse me?" Erin says quietly. I watch her leave and feel the natural urge to run after her, but I think she needs space and wouldn't appreciate my hovering. The family regards our interaction with questions marring each of their faces. I can't help but sigh.

"Can we meet in Mohan's office?" I mutter. "We have some things to discuss."

The family finishes their breakfast quickly and makes their way to the office. I don't intend to tell them about Erin's mistake, but they need to know about the dreams.

My mother pulls me to one side before I have the chance to follow. "Is Erin okay?"

I shake my head. "Would you go after her? I think she would benefit from a chat with you."

"Of course. See you soon."

Putting my feelings to one side, I square my shoulders. Everyone is settled when I enter and shut the door. "I have some news."

I tell them about the dreams and the rocky outcrop. Marcus instantly reaches for a pad and pen.

"Could you draw it?" he asks.

"Well, I'm no Van Gogh, but I'll try."

As I do my best to draw the rocks, the rest of the family discusses the dreams and their significance between themselves. I'm not sure how much time has passed. I smile when the door opens, revealing my mother and a smiling Erin. She marches straight over to me and kisses me to within an inch of my life.

Blinking like an idiot, I can't help the goofy grin that is plastered on my face. She takes my breath away every time. I ignore the scoff and gagging noise from Lucille.

"Hello, my love," I finally say.

Perching on my knee, Erin surveys the drawing. Plucking the pen from my hand, she adds a few missing details.

"There, that's almost a perfect likeness." She hands it over to Marcus, who sets to work immediately.

"Once we find the location, what's the plan?" Laurence asks.

Good question. I already know what Erin will want to do.

"We go there," she says without a second's pause.

"Sounds easy enough." Aliah laughs.

"We will need to plan. Wherever it is—"

"Borneo," Marcus announces. "It's in Borneo, look." He holds his phone up to my face and shows me the rock formation. "Isn't the internet a wonderful thing?" He chuckles.

"So, we're going to Borneo," I say.

"We are, and as soon as possible," Erin replies. "The key to stopping the president is there. I know it."

Disregarding this morning, I trust Erin with my life. If she thinks that hut will somehow stop the slaughter of our people, I will support her all the way.

"I suggest you take this to Mohan and the council members."

"I'm not asking permission," Erin shoots. Her fiery side really gets me going.

Father holds up his hand. "I'm not saying that. I just think we should be transparent. Keep everyone in the loop."

"He's right, love. There's no need to keep this a secret."

Erin eyes me and then looks sheepish. "Sorry, Harlan. I didn't mean to jump down your throat."

Father lets out a deep laugh. "I do love your sassy side, little one."

Erin squints her eyes at him playfully. "I might be little, but I could still take you, old man."

The family laughs along.

"I have no doubts," he bellows. It's nice to have a bit of fun.

"Alright, let's gather everyone up. No reason to wait. Time is of the essence," Mother calls, clapping her hands.

I take Valentine in my arms while the room erupts into chatter and discussion. I can't remember the last time I got to hold my baby sister. She's another dark-haired beauty who has captured the hearts of everyone in the bunker. I feel I've missed out on so much time with her.

I hate she's had nothing but upheaval since she was born. First Noah, and now the fucking President of the United States. On the bright side, her social skills will be off the charts. I'm sure everyone here has offered to look after her at one time or another.

Looking into her eyes, I can't help but envision my own child. I ache to make it a reality. I see myself holding a blonde-haired, blue-eyed, sassy little tyke who takes after Erin. She'd have me wrapped around her little finger from her first breath.

In all the chaos, we've never gotten around to seriously discussing children. We both want them, but that's as far as we got. Some part of me thought about holding off. Like my parents. But now? I want to start a family as soon as possible. Life is unpredictable, and I don't want to waste a second of it.

"You look deep in thought, honey," Erin says as she kisses Valentine on the head. My sister reaches for her instantly. Erin scoops her out of my arms and holds her tight.

"I was thinking about children." Erin's eyes snap to mine. "I know it's not exactly the ideal time to talk about it."

"We can talk about it whenever you want."

I watch Valentine play with Erin's golden locks. "I want that. I want to watch our baby girl play with your hair. I want to look into beautiful little eyes that remind me of her mother."

"I'm ready, Amelia. You only have to say the word. I want nothing more than to have a family with you."

I smile and kiss her gently. "When all this is over, and we've taken a really long vacation. I'd like to do it."

"I can't wait," she replies, rubbing her nose against mine. Mohan's clapping draws our attention.

"Quiet, please. Quiet." It only takes a few moments for silence to descend. "Okay, I think between us all we can get you both to Borneo," he says, looking at me and Erin.

"We need to take precautions, but I'm confident we can get the job done."

"Thank you, Mohan," Erin says. "Thank you everyone. I know this isn't easy."

Mohan bows. "We trust you, my Queen."

I'm about to reply when there is a commotion. All attention turns toward the door. Chris bursts through the crowd, his face etched in fear.

"Erin!" He gasps. "Mack..." Bending over, he tries to suck in some much-needed air. Erin passes Valentine to my mother and is by his side in a second, guiding him to a chair.

"Deep breaths, Chris."

"They've been taken! Mack and Jordan."

"Taken?" Erin says, a quiver in her voice.

Christopher nods rapidly. "We didn't see them coming. It was a trap. It was chaos, Erin. We got split up, but I saw it. I saw Mack and Jordan stuffed into the back of a van. I tried to get to them. I swear I did," he cries. Erin looks at me with wide eyes. Unshed tears gather, waiting to spill over.

My warrior wakes up, ready to burn the world down to find our friends. I temper the urge but keep her close to the surface. This is my purpose.

"Chris, where were you?" I ask. His shaking fingers take out the map, which pinpointed the different rendezvous points the trio planned to visit. He points to one in LA.

Fuck.

Out of all the places, LA is the most dangerous for us to be. Our whole lives were there and therefore it stands to reason it would be the first place the Special Forces will stake out.

"We have to find them," Erin chokes.

I know Mack and Jordan's kidnapping will hit her the hardest. Especially Jordan, who she still shares a connection with. Mack and I have the same bond, but weaker. Regardless, she's still a part of me and I have to find her.

"Erin, can you reach Jordan?"

Her body is shaking, but she closes her eyes and tries to connect. Tears spill as she shakes her head. "Nothing. I can't reach her—"

"If I had to take a guess," Dr. Chord interjects. "I'd say they were tranquilized."

I have never been happier to see another vampire. The last time we saw Dr. Chord, she was helping us with the

Noah situation. She also milked me, allowing more Fallen to get help faster.

Mohan and the family pull her into a hug. When she reaches me, I take her hand and bow my head. If anyone deserves praise and adulation, it's her. Any doctor, actually.

"It's wonderful to see you, Doctor."

"I'm sorry it took so long to get here. There were people in need along the way. As soon as I ran out of your venom, I came here as fast as I could."

"We'll set up a time to give you more. Right now, we need to come up with a plan to be in two places at once." Erin looks at me, confused. "Going to Borneo is still a priority. But now we have another. Retrieving Mack and Jordan."

"What are you suggesting?" Mother asks.

I can't believe I'm going to say this, but it's the only way. "Erin will go to Borneo, and I will find our friends."

"You want to split up?" Erin asks, fire in her voice.

"It's the only way. We are running out of time, my love."

Fourteen

ERIN

I never thought I'd say this, but she's out of her fucking mind! Split up? Is she high? Actually, I'd quite like to be high right now. Maybe I wouldn't feel as if I'm about to have a coronary then. Obviously, I keep all those thoughts locked inside as I glare at Amelia. The Salvator Regina can't cuss like that. I know I'm not a real queen, but some of these vampires look at me like I'm royalty and a part of me doesn't want to disappoint.

"We need to talk about this," I say as calmly as possible. *Now!* I demand not so calmly in my mind.

She sighs but nods. "Mohan, will you get as much information from Chris as possible," she says in a low voice. "We'll be back in a minute."

"Good luck," Lucille titters as Amelia follows me back to our room. The second our door closes, I round on her.

"There's no fucking way we are splitting up, Amelia. I can't believe you even suggested it!"

"Erin—" she says in a placating tone that only ruffles my feathers all the more.

"No. Don't *Erin* me, Amelia Loch. You shouldn't have even uttered the words until you'd run the idea past me."

"We haven't got time to come up with another plan, Erin. Trust me, I hate the idea of being apart as much as you do. My purpose in life is to keep you safe, but I know deep inside this is the right thing to do. You have to find that hut. We need answers, but we both know Mack and Jordan need to be found ASAP. God knows what's happening to them."

"Of course I know that!" My voice is loud. "It's breaking me apart, knowing I didn't feel Jordan was in trouble." I can't believe I didn't have even an inkling they were in danger. Another thing to feel shitty about. "I want nothing more than to find them, but we are strongest together. Haven't we proven that time and time again?"

We have overcome every obstacle because we were together. This is the biggest obstacle we've ever faced. How can she think anything but sticking together is right?

"Yes, but we've also come a long way since our change. We grow stronger every day. You are probably the most powerful vampire of our time. I know we can help each other even from far apart. You must feel it? We can bridge any distance. I'd find you through time and space, Erin. That's how much faith I have in us."

Damn it, she has a point. And she's hot as fuck when she gets passionate. *Not the time.*

"I don't like this," I growl.

Amelia moves to me, her arms surrounding me, grounding me. I've been pacing the length of the room without realizing.

"We have to believe in our abilities and the people around us. Splitting up doesn't mean I intend to ship you off to the jungle alone, my love. You know that would never happen."

"So, we form teams?"

"Yes. We're not alone in this fight."

"Swear to me, you'll be careful, Amelia. I know your warrior, and how she likes to run headfirst into situations. We don't know what we're facing."

"I promise. We won't take any unnecessary risks, but there is a strong possibility I'll have to fight. Whoever has Jordan and Mack won't want to give them up easily."

My mind wanders back to Amelia's previous worries regarding her restraint. She looks so assured within herself now.

"I'm in control," she says, placing a kiss on my lips. "I've had a word with my warrior. She knows who's boss."

I deflate with resignation. I'm not going to change her mind, and after talking it through, I'm not even sure I should.

"Let's address the others. We can't run off half-cocked. I know time is against us, but we must have a solid plan, Amelia."

"Agreed. Come on, let's get this party started."

"We have very different interpretations of a party, my love."

She chuckles as she pulls me back to the common room. Christopher looks better but is still shaken. His eyes are glassy and his skin pale. All eyes turn to us as we re-enter.

"It's decided. Amelia will search for Jordan and Mack. I will travel to Borneo."

"I volunteer to go with you," Lucille says. I should have known she would want to take Amelia's place as my protector. No matter how much they argue and fight, Amelia and Lucille have the same heart. "I'll keep you safe."

I take her hand and squeeze. Amelia is glowing with love and pride. I'll remind them of this when they decide to rip chunks out of each other.

"Me too," Marcus calls. "I'm pretty sure I can help with navigation. Plus, I've been doing some research on the area."

"Thank you," I say.

"May I offer my help to you, Amelia?" Mr. Becker asks as he steps through the crowd. "I may not have your power, but I can hold my own."

"It would be an honor, thank you," Amelia says. Even though they had a rough start, I think they will become fast friends. Mr. Becker has earned Amelia's respect and vice versa.

"Then please call me Simon."

"Simon. Okay."

Paula and Ricco step forward, offering their help. In less than ten minutes, we have two strong and capable teams. Even though we are still in the same room, the distance seems to have already grown between Amelia and me.

"We'll go to the gym area," Amelia says quietly. "A few hours and then we'll be together."

"For now," I reply with a tremble in my voice. "Tomorrow will come fast and then I don't know when we'll see each other again."

Tomorrow isn't a fixed deadline to leave, but I know it won't be much later.

She takes me in her arms regardless of the spectators. "I'm with you always," she says with her smooth, silky voice, placing her hand on my heart. "In here," she shifts her hand to my cheek, "and in here."

"I love you."

"I love you, too. Now, let's get to planning so I can take you to bed and show you how much."

We break apart. I follow my group to Mohan's office. My heart is beating hard with the knowledge that Amelia is leaving me. I know it's not like *that*. But I also know my place is by her side, and any other scenario feels wrong.

"Let's get this done," Lucille says with her usual brashness. "Right now, you need to be the Salvator Regina, not Erin, okay?"

"Okay."

Marcus is already bending over a map. "I've traced the rock formation to Mulu National Park," he says, jabbing a spot on the paper. "I suggest that's where we start."

"What's the plan when we arrive? If I'm not mistaken, it's a rather extensive area to search," Lucille asks.

"Oh yeah, it's huge," Marcus replies.

I clear my throat. "I believe I can guide us once we are there."

"What do you think we'll find?" Paula asks. I was pleasantly surprised when Paula and Ricco offered to come along.

Shrugging my shoulders, I fiddle with the edge of the map. "I honestly don't know. You should all know before we set off that this could lead to nothing. I don't think that will be the case, but there is a possibility."

"But you feel it, right? In your gut?" Ricco asks.

"I do."

"That's all we need to know then," Marcus says. "Could it be a weapon of some sort?"

"Maybe."

Jesus, I wish I could offer them more than that.

"We don't want to start a war though," Lucille remarks, rubbing her chin. "Whatever we find, we'd be remiss to use it blindly. This is a delicate situation. Our lives depend on a peaceful resolution."

"I agree." And I really do. If we find something that will only exacerbate things between us and the humans, I won't use it. "We'll bring whatever we find back to the bunker and discuss its usefulness with the council."

Marcus packs away the map. "I'll find Mohan and start arranging travel. I don't think we can do a straight run. A few stops might be better."

"Do whatever you need to do. Everyone else, gather your belongings and say goodbye to your loved ones. We go as soon as we have transport."

Instead of driving myself nuts waiting for Amelia in our room, I find Victoria, Harlan, and little Valentine. Choosing to concentrate on the conversation Amelia and I had about kids is a much better way to pass the time than slowly going nuts with worry.

We play peek-a-boo, hide-and-go-seek, and "bonk daddy on the head with a stuffed toy." The latter is definitely her favorite. It still shocks me a little that Victoria and Harlan are parents again at 200 years old. I just can't wrap my head around it.

"She adores you," Victoria says, coming over to sit with Valentine and me on the ground. She's constructing some sort of fort with blocks. It's quite impressive.

"I adore her. Look at her. She reminds me of Amelia."

Victoria laughs. "Oh, she's just like her older sister. Temperament and all. Like Lucille too, although a little less volatile."

I can't help but chuckle. Of course, Lucille was a little hellion.

"I can't wait to have our own little Amelia. Although she wants a mini-Erin."

"You can have scores of both if you want. I won't complain. I love being a grandparent as much as a mother."

"One day," I say wistfully. "For now, I'm concentrating on getting through the next twenty-four hours."

"You're both strong enough, Erin. This is but a blip on your timeline. You will have infinity together if you wish. I know you hate being apart, but Amelia is right. This is the right course of action. Plus, you can be with her anytime you want. That's the advantage of the gift of telepathy."

Scoffing, I shake my head. "I'm not in a rush to do that again."

Victoria was good enough to talk me out of my slump earlier. I told her about hijacking Amelia's mind and how disgusted I felt with myself once I realized the impact of what I had done. She didn't excuse me, but she understood the situation I was in.

"Nonsense. It was a mistake. Move on. Amelia would be devastated if she heard you talking that way about a transgression."

"I know. I'll get over it, eventually."

"Make the most of your bond, Erin. And make the most of tonight. Reaffirm your connection with your mate, and that will carry you through the hard times, I promise."

Leaning over, I embrace Victoria. "Thank you. I don't know what I would do without you sometimes."

"You'll never have to know. You're as much a daughter to me as the rest of them."

Sucking in a deep breath, I stand. "I'm going to say goodbye to Mom and Dad, and then I'm going to find my wife."

"Atta girl." Victoria grins.

Saying goodbye to my parents goes better than expected. They've grown thick skins since my change.

I know they lean heavily on the Lochs to help them understand what I go through, and I'm grateful. I don't have to worry about them anymore.

Finally, back in our room, I strip, shower, and lay myself on the bed. I'm done waiting. I need Amelia here, on me, inside me. I need to know everything will be okay.

Expanding my mind, I let my soul reach out. Pouring every bit of love and lust I have into my aura, I feel my skin glow as gold threads twist and turn toward the door. They're searching for her. The second Amelia feels me, I ignite. Her excitement is palpable.

We're going to set this place on fire tonight. I hope the walls are soundproof.

Fifteen

AMELIA

A thrill courses through my body. It's equal parts lust for my wife, who is waiting for me to return to our room so we can devour each other, and anticipation for the task at hand. I shouldn't be excited about leaving, especially when Erin won't be with me, but I'd be lying if I said the idea of hunting down the people who took Mack and Jordan isn't lighting me up like the Fourth of July.

My time spent in the gym with my team consisted of strategizing and training. There isn't much to plan until we reach the area where our friends were taken. I'm positive I'll be able to pick up their scent. No one has senses like mine. The actual planning will come into play when we have their location. No doubt some military black site with security up the wazoo. But that's something to deal with later.

Sparring was fun and I'm more than impressed by Simon's moves. He's a fast learner. Chris will also join us, and I already know he can handle himself. Hell, he was able to wrangle me when I went full monster at Mack's place.

Knowing our team is solid meant I had no worries dismissing them the second Erin opened herself up to me. The wave of love and lust smashed into me with the force of a hurricane. I couldn't get to her fast enough.

Opening the door to our room, I brace myself. I expect to see her lying on the bed, naked and wanting. But expectation and reality are two different things. My wife is crouched on the bed, a look of pure animalistic hunger literally shining off her in gold ribbons. The second the door clicks shut, she launches herself at me. For a small woman, she's got the most powerful legs I've ever seen. I catch her easily, but the sheer force of her momentum slams me back into the door with a loud thud that echoes around the room.

Fangs pierce my neck, and I'm flooded with adrenaline. My panties are ruined. My nails instinctively drag down her back, causing her to moan. I love it when we have sex like this. Totally unencumbered by anything. One hundred percent in the moment, happy to give each other anything we want and need. And right now, Erin needs to feel in control. She needs her base instincts catered to, and I'm fine with that.

Pushing off the door, I spin and pin her back forcefully. Her head snaps up from my neck. Two rivulets of blood drip from her fangs. I can't help but remember the first time she bit me. Her utter mortification was so strong, she fled out of fear. Well now, fang play is one of the most erotic things either of us can experience. It's not always called for. When we make soft, unhurried love, our blood play doesn't feel appropriate. But when we feel raw passion like now, I fucking love biting her and vice versa. It's a shot of power straight to the clit.

My tongue traces her fangs, making her growl. Squeezing her ass, I pull her legs wider, allowing me to push my hips as close as possible. Her pussy is dripping, and I know the coarse fabric of my pants is already stimulating her. With a few hard rolls, Erin starts to pant, but I'm not ready for her to come yet. I want us to climax together. I want our auras to dance, lighting up the room with gold and blue. It's our own private firework display that announces to the universe we are made for this. Made for each other.

Erin lets out a little squeak of surprise when I suddenly turn us and throw her onto the bed. She lands with a soft thud and her hands grab the bedspread. Taking two strides forward, I wait at the end of the bed. I'm slowing things down a little, but that doesn't mean I won't extract every ounce of pleasure from her. I just want her to savor this moment as I undress.

The second my panties hit the floor, she reaches for me, but I command her to stop. I can smell her arousal, and I know it's running down her legs.

"On your back, Erin." Of course she doesn't protest.

Walking over to the bedside table, I extract two playthings. Her eyes are like fire when she sees what we will play with. I hand my favorite plug to her and keep hold of Erin's favorite dildo. With no more time to lose, I straddle her, bringing my aching clitoris mere centimeters from her mouth. I unconsciously lick my lips when I peer down at her silky, wet folds. So ready for a tongue lashing.

We've done every position thinkable, but the tried and tested 69 is my favorite when it comes to giving each other simultaneous pleasure. Especially with toys added into the mix.

Erin is impatient and swipes her tongue over the entirety of my slit. My head drops as I experience every last millisecond of it. I'm done going slow now. Placing the dildo on the bed, I grab her thighs, curling her body toward me. She's so open, so ready. With a growl, I delve in, eating her as if it's the last thing I will ever have in my mouth. Erin follows suit and together we feast. When I feel her legs begin to shake, I tear my mouth away, laughing at her protest. She won't be upset for long.

The dildo springs to life with the push of a button. I set it on a low pulse. There's no way she's coming so easily. I'm going to edge the shit out of her until she's so frustrated she sinks her fangs into me again. The toy slips easily inside. It's big and stretches her wide. For a few moments, I simply watch as it disappears with ease. My own pleasure forgotten as I stare entranced. That is, until the icy trickle of lube down my ass makes me jump. I hear a little titter, but that's okay. She can have her fun.

Erin delicately slides the plug in, giving me time to adjust. As soon as she feels me relax, she activates the vibration. I have to screw my eyes shut and concentrate hard not to come.

When I feel under control, I get back to work. Erin is as relentless as I am, and together we pound, lick, suck, and fuck until we're both quivering messes. Finally, Erin becomes so frustrated she does the one thing I crave. Her fangs slice through my inner thigh. I can't help the scream that slips from my throat. The only thing I can do is reciprocate. I want her to have the same rush as me, the one that will inevitably tip us over the edge. My climax is ferocious and loud. The room is alive with color. It's almost blinding. The shockwaves continue on and on. I feel Erin's body convulse below me until we both collapse, completely spent and sated.

As I pant, in a desperate bid to draw air into my lungs, I feel my soul bask in Erin and our connection. I have never felt stronger than at this minute.

We are unstoppable.

I'm woken with light fingertips caressing my stomach. Erin's contented sigh washes over my skin like a warm summer breeze. At this moment, I don't want to leave. I want to stay right here, with my mate wrapped up in my arms, ignoring the rest of the world.

"Good morning, my love," I say, kissing the top of her head. She shifts to look up at me and what I see makes it hard to breathe. Tears brim on the edge of falling. There is nothing I can say that will make her feel better. The next few days, possibly weeks, are going to be some of the toughest we've ever faced. So, instead of words, I pull her closer and claim her lips. It's passion and pent-up fear rolled into one.

When we finally part, I swipe a rogue tear from her beautiful face. "Last night was exquisite."

She nods. "It was everything I needed."

"Me too. And I feel powerful."

It's no lie. I can still feel our souls pulsating with energy. The kind of energy that could destroy worlds. Maybe I should fear our ability to summon such a force, but I don't. There is no fear when I know the hearts that lay below our chests are good and pure. We only want to help.

"Your mom told me to make every second of our last night together count."

"Do we have to bring up my mother when we're lying here naked, honey?"

For the first time in days, she gives me a genuine laugh. "Sorry. I just wanted you to know that I gave you everything I had last night. Not just sexually—although you *did* ring me dry. I mean every bit of love and power I have. I wanted you to have it."

"I know, and I hope I did the same. No matter what, Erin, we will be together again. The universe wills it."

She grins at me. "I love it when you get all hocus pocus on me. Maybe I can find a way to show your past self. I think she'd find it amusing."

Rolling my eyes, I tickle her until she screams. "I was different back then."

"We both were."

"Do you ever regret it?"

"It?"

I inhale her scent. "Me. Do you ever regret meeting me?"

She bolts upright until her face is directly in front of me. "Never. I'd go through it all again, a thousand times over Amelia Loch."

"But you would live a peaceful life. None of this." I wave my hand around, vaguely gesturing to our concrete prison.

"I would miss out on the one thing that makes me whole. Do you regret meeting me?"

"Don't utter such words. I can't bear to hear them."

"Exactly. No more of that."

We go silent, gazing at each other, memorizing this moment.

"Are you ready?"

She strokes my cheek. "As ready as I can be."

"What time do you have to go?" I know Erin will leave tomorrow. My team will head out tonight.

"I'm waiting for an exact time. Do you have everything you need?"

"Yes."

"We've still got a few hours, my love."

"Then let's not waste a second."

And we don't. Hours slip by as we dedicate our attention to each other. It's only when Mother knocks on our door that we pull apart. The time is upon us, and I'm not sure how I go about saying goodbye.

"We don't say goodbye," Erin says softly. Clearly my emotions are running rampant and she's picking up my thoughts. "We kiss and we hug, then we say, I love you, and nothing more."

"Okay," I croak.

We shower and dress in silence. Chris and Simon are waiting by the exit door, their packs resting at their feet. My family swarm around us as soon as we step into the room. In some ways, I wish I could have snuck out. Saying tearful goodbyes to my siblings and parents is depleting my courage and willingness to leave. Erin must sense my struggle because she pulls me away and over to my team. Gone are her sorrowful eyes. The Salvator Regina stands before me now, and I'm so very grateful. Seeing her like this kicks my warrior into high gear, reminding me of what I have to do. Not just for Mack and Jordan, but for her.

I have to fight for our freedom, and I have to fight for the safety of my mate, my Queen. I kiss her soundly before making eye contact with the Loch clan. With a single nod, I hike up my pack and turn away. Chris and Simon follow suit, their resolve as steadfast as my own.

I embrace the cool night air, letting it fill my lungs. God, it feels good to be in the world again. I flex my body, feeling Erin's strength saturating my muscles.

I am ready.

<h1 style="text-align:center">Sixteen</h1>

ERIN

I'm making the conscious decision to grow a pair of steel ovaries. Wallowing isn't helpful to anyone. I cannot fall apart just because Amelia has gone. She wouldn't want that. I have every faith she will return Mack and Jordan to us safely. There are too many vampires relying on us to let my heartache interfere with our plans. So, I'll buck up.

If I want Amelia back in my arms, we need to find out what the hell is in that jungle, pronto. I'm still certain it holds the key to solving our presidential issue. Every time I experience a sliver of doubt, I recall hearing my name being called on the wind, reaffirming my belief.

Low chatter rumbles behind me, reminding me I'm in a room full of expectant vampires. They're waiting to see how their "Queen" conducts herself. Pulling my shoulders back, I turn to face the crowd.

"Have we got everything ready to go?" I ask no one in particular. Getting down to business is a necessity. I'm tired of waiting. If I could run out of the bunker this second and get on with the journey, I would.

Lucille steps forward. "We're traveling light. Everyone has one small backpack. Mohan has arranged for Jeremy to pick us up at 8 a.m."

It made sense to utilize Jeremy's services again. It's unlikely that a government vehicle will get pulled over.

"Excellent. I suggest we get some rest and food. It's going to be a long night."

With that, I excuse myself. Unlike my team, I have not readied my pack. I just couldn't bring myself to do it with Amelia still here. We had more important things to do, like making love until our bodies were exhausted. Now there's no excuse. However, I'm not convinced the meager clothing I have with me is very suitable for the jungle. Hawaii didn't exactly require that I pack camo trousers. I'm guessing they would be the appropriate pants, right? Funnily enough, being an excellent mixologist doesn't lend itself to these types of adventures. I am wildly out of my comfort zone.

Picking up my well-worn Insomnia T-shirt brings me some comfort as I pull it to my face and inhale like a lunatic. Whatever, it makes me feel better smelling my home and Amelia. She likes me in this particular shirt because it's tight across my chest. Yes, my wife is quite the perv.

Enough of that.

Okay, so I have a t-shirt. That's a start. I fish through a mountain of bikinis and sarongs. Neither are making the cut. I have a few pairs of shorts, but they are linen. Sure, they'll be lightweight, but I'm guessing bugs will eat my legs alive. Damn, if Amelia were coming with me, I could've asked her to throw one of her protective shields around me, therefore saving my skin from becoming a mosquito's banquet.

Slumping on the bed, I can't help but sigh. This is going to be tougher than I thought. I need to have absolute focus. But right now, that feels impossible. I'm saved from my black hole by Lucille pushing through the door. She has zero respect or boundaries sometimes.

"Here," she says, thrusting a pile of fabric at me. "I took the liberty of getting some shit together for you."

Camo pants, socks, sports bra, and t-shirts. It's everything I need. "Thank you."

Lucille comes further into the room and sits on the end of the bed. "You know I'll keep you safe, right?"

"Of course I do."

She nods. "Good. Although you're stronger than you know, Erin. I don't want you going into this thing feeling anything but confident in your ability to get this done."

She's very sweet sometimes. I won't verbalize that because she'll probably hit me or something, but still, Lucille Loch is a real softy under all those prickles.

"I have to say I'm feeling a little less confident without your sister by my side."

"Understandable. But your abilities are far superior. And I'm not saying that because Amelia annoys the shit out of me." She grins. "Your power comes from wielding your mind, which is so much more devastating than hitting and kicking your way through a situation. Remember what you can do, okay? There isn't a person, human or vampire alive that can match you. So, if anything happens when we're out there, don't hesitate to call on your inner queen. Erin, use what you've been given."

"I don't want to hurt anyone, Luce. That's not why I have these gifts."

She takes my hand. "I know that. I'm not asking you to go all bat shit crazy, but make sure you defend yourself to the best of your ability. That's all I ask."

My heart rate is picking up. I swallow thickly. "Do you think I'm leading us all into a trap or something?"

"No. I don't. But we're living in unstable times, and I want you to be vigilant. I'm more worried about getting to the jungle than I am finding out what's led us there."

"The travel plans seem solid enough."

"They are. However, the Special Forces have taken us by surprise before."

Of course, she's referring to the fact our friends were taken, and we had no forewarning. There are supposed to be vampires close to the Commander-in-Chief. They have been our source of information, and yet no one warned us. Which can only mean the Special Forces are keeping their ability to find us close to the chest. I can only imagine they have specialized equipment. Facial recognition software, possibly. It would make sense they went looking for Mack considering she's our friend. That's worrying.

"I'll be alert and ready," I say. I home in on the well of power still clinging to my cells. Amelia's strength lives within my tissue.

I can do this.

Lucille leaves as soon as she is sure I am as ready as I claim. The fact is, I am stronger than anyone we know. To the best of my knowledge, I, like Amelia, cannot be killed by conventional methods. I can infiltrate the mind of my foe if necessary, just like I did with Noah. There really is no reason for me to panic, and yet a small part of me is. I'll chalk it up to the part of me that still feels like the old Erin Hanson, a small and vulnerable human.

Walking to the bathroom, I stare at my reflection in the floor-length mirror. I'm still short. I still have that sassy fire burning in my eyes. It's just a little more intense now. Deep down, I *am* still the same vulnerable person, and I like that. It keeps me grounded. In contrast, though, I am so much more than I was. My body is firmer, my mind stronger. I am Erin Hanson 2.0.

And then I hear her. *You are everything.*

The goodbye was as awful as I thought it would be. Nearly every vampire in the bunker came to wish us well on our journey. I honestly could have done without that. Thankfully, Lucille was her usual acerbic self and practically bulldozed her way through the crowd, dragging me with her. I'm sure I saw a few people topple over as she broke through. I said goodbye to my parents and the Loch clan earlier in the evening and in private. It was intense, but they gave me even more strength to draw from. I know they will all be okay.

Jeremy welcomed us with a handshake. I presume he's on a need-to-know basis, and all he needs to know is we have to get to a private airport three hundred miles away by 2 p.m.

I'm in the back with Paula and Ricco. They've kept me distracted with stories of their life. Lucille is upfront with Jeremy. I can't help but chuckle when Jeremy does his utmost to engage Lucille in conversation. She's as stoney faced as ever. Marcus is in the rear, with maps strewn out on either side of him. The man must have learned everything there is to know about Borneo. He's mapped out our route in painstaking detail. I also notice he has several backup routes plotted. I have to give it to the Loch siblings. They don't do anything half-ass. I say that knowing that Lucille has concealed many, *many* weapons on her body. She's a bitchy Rambo, and I love it. We're prepared.

I try to reach Jordan and Mack now and then, but I'm still finding nothing but darkness. Whatever the military is drugging them with is highly effective. Amelia is easier to connect to. I don't initiate a conversation because I don't want to distract her, but a quick check-in is enough to satisfy me. She's safe. In fact, I've got the distinct impression she's rather enjoying herself, which is interesting. It would take me but a second to look through her eyes and see what she's up to, but I've learned my lesson. I'll wait until she wants to share with me freely.

Mohan enters my mind and updates me on his task to reach the White House informant. Apparently, the president is keeping everything to herself. She's not even confiding in her inner circle. Mohan tells me the Special Forces believe they are rounding up terrorists. I'm relieved, if I'm being honest. This way, if we can get to the president and convince her to stop hunting us, the fallout is minimal. Lord knows how we would go about trying to contain our identity if a bunch of other bureaucrats and military officials knew of our existence.

The roads are empty as we drive. As predicted, we don't encounter any issues and arrive at the airfield with half an hour to spare. This is where the comfort ends, though. Going forward, we will ride in tiny ass planes under false identities that will drop us off at random airfields all over the planet. I'm not even being dramatic. It's going to take us days to arrive in Borneo.

I give Jeremy a hug before heading over to our tiny plane. I'm not usually a nervous flier, but then again, I'm not used to flying in a toy aircraft. Jesus, the thing looks like a stiff wind could snap it in two.

Things get even worse when Lucille hops into the pilot seat. I've seen her drive a car. It's traumatic. Crap, I should have taken some Valium or at least stashed a hipflask.

My leg bounces as I watch her do pre-flight checks. Marcus is also looking a little concerned. I catch his eye, and he raises both eyebrows. That can't be good, right?

"Um, so how long have you been a pilot?" I ask.

"Long enough," Lucille replies, effectively shutting the conversation down. I tug on my harness several times to make sure it's secure. Not sure it will do much good if we plummet to the ground. The engines fire up and I send a quick "I love you" to Amelia.

The entire body of the plane is shaking as we make our way down the tarmac. Lucille garbles into the headset and then throws the throttle down. I'm catapulted back into my seat. Lucille lets out a manic laugh as we careen forward, picking up speed. Paula whoops in excitement. I have a feeling she'll change her attitude once we're up in the air. Lucille is a menace behind the wheel, and I bet that extends to any type of vehicle.

Sure enough, every passenger is green by the time we land. I can't believe we have to do this multiple times. Lucille is practically giddy, and either hasn't noticed us, or most likely, doesn't give a rat's ass about our current welfare. Yeah, it's definitely the latter.

We only have fifteen minutes to get our belongings together and get them transferred to a car waiting for us by the small hangar. Mohan and the council pulled in every favor to get us securely out of the country. I really hope we don't mess up.

Seventeen

AMELIA

The first few hours of our escapade would have taken several years off my life if I weren't immortal. I'd forgotten how stressful it was evading the military.

Thankfully, the secluded area of the bunker and cabin allowed us to move undetected. Unless there were military scoping out the National Forest with night vision goggles, we knew we wouldn't run into trouble. No matter how many times I repeated that to myself, though, I couldn't help but freeze at every sound. For once, my enhanced hearing didn't help. Unbelievable for the Salvator Regina's mate, right? I mean, how ridiculous. Erin and I escaped Hawaii and made it to the mainland. *After* subduing several soldiers. And yet here I am, traveling through the forest and mountains, jumping out of my skin every fifty yards. It takes a harsh self-talking to before I get myself under control. I believe my warrior would smack me upside the head if possible.

Things get tense when we emerge from the safety of the park. That's when the real journey begins. It's also when I nearly squeal with excitement when I see two Ducati motorbikes stashed away. It feels like a lifetime since I've had so much mechanical power between my thighs. My adrenaline spikes before I've even thrown my leg over the machine.

I won't even question how Mohan arranged it. Simon is more than happy to ride on the back of Chris's bike, leaving me to enjoy the ride alone. We hit the deserted highway, and I let all my pent-up frustration out on the throttle. God, it feels amazing. We hit speeds that Erin would chastise me for, even though she secretly loves the thrill herself.

We finally pull over. Tiredness is a killer, and we've been going full-on for hours. Chris reassures me we will be at the rendezvous point in just a couple more hours. I'm itching to get going, but Simon and Chris are insisting we take a longer break.

"I do love pancakes," Chris says through mouthfuls of food. The greasy diner is half empty, but we still eat next to the bikes. I'd rather not take the chance. Simon was happy to collect the food, given that Chris and I are bigger targets. Does that sound paranoid?

"Nah, it's fried chicken for me," Simon says, shoving an entire pancake in his mouth. "But these are pretty good."

"Tapas. That's my favourite food," I say. "Ham croquettes, mmm, delicious."

"Do you ever wonder how different food tastes to a human? I know we eat like them, but do you think their tastebuds find food tastier?" Simon remarks. I wonder if this is the first time he's really contemplated our species differences. I can hazard a guess that the newly reformed asshole never dealt with humans much.

"Haven't you got human friends?" Chris asks.

Simon shakes his head. "I can't say I wanted to interact with them much. My father ran our business, and I...well, I'm a little embarrassed to say I rode his coattails. I lounged around all day to be honest. Terrible, isn't it? I'm a council member, but even that only happened because of my father's influence."

"Do you like being a council member?" I ask.

He shrugs. "I don't really do much. Sure, I sit in on meetings and help with decision making, but I'm on the bottom of the totem pole."

I ball up my paper and throw it in the nearest bin. It's a three-pointer for sure. Didn't even touch the rim. "And when we get back? When all this is over with?"

Simon's shoulders pull back, a smile stretches across his face. "I think I want to open a gym." Well, I wasn't expecting that. "What about you? Now you're a queen."

I scoff. "Erin and I will go back to serving drinks and living a peaceful existence."

Chris eyes me thoughtfully. "You really think you can just go back to everyday life?"

"Yes." I will make damn sure of it. "Now, are you ready to get going?"

They polish off the rest of their breakfast in two giant mouthfuls.

"How much is it eating you up to have us weighing you down?" Chris laughs. "I bet you'd already be there by now if left to your own devices. Shit, you could have probably run the whole way just as fast as we're riding."

I grin. "I've never tried to run that far. I'll make a note to test myself."

Simon looks at me wide eyed. "So, all the rumors are true? About your abilities."

"Don't listen to rumors." I laugh. "Right, let's do this. The longer it takes, the less chance I'll have at picking up a scent."

We hop on our bikes and rev the engines. It's childish, but it makes me happy. Mother would love it.

My merriment fizzles as we enter LA. Of all the places to go, this is the worst. It's like I can feel eyes on me. Chris takes the lead, weaving us through the streets and back alleys. We pull over again, but this time we won't be having a casual chit chat over food. We're three blocks from the rendezvous point. I didn't want to risk us getting any closer without surveilling the area first.

Lucille gave me a stack of clothes and a dark baseball cap before I left, which I found a little creepy at the time. Like, does she just have a random closet of dark camos and t-shirts knocking about? And if she does, why?

Anyway, at least I'm in comfortable clothing. I wasn't looking forward to traveling in short shorts and a bikini top. And I'd been wearing my travel clothes for weeks. Damn, I should have made sure Erin was equipped before I left.

I feel her presence. *Lucille came to the rescue.*

Okay, so Erin is fine. Back to the task at hand. For this, I need to go alone. I can scan the buildings and streets much faster by myself.

"Wait here. Don't move, I'll be quick."

"Be safe," Chris whispers.

"You too. Do. Not. Move!"

We're in a rundown part of town. I can't help but calculate the distance from here to Insomnia. If I didn't think Erin and the rest of my family would crucify me, I'd run over and take a look at my beloved club.

I need to focus. Shoving everything to the back of my mind, I bring my senses forward. My ear picks up the rats scuttling around. I hear a heartbeat down the alley two blocks away. By the smell, it's a homeless person. Scaling the closest building, I crouch down on the roof, allowing my eyes to adjust to the early morning light. I can see the building where Mack and Jordan were taken from. Scanning the closest buildings, I'm satisfied there are no soldiers. I take a huge whiff of the air, dissecting every smell. LA is utterly disgusting to inhale, but I'm confident no one of any threat is lurking around.

We only have a short time before the city comes alive. Jumping down, I land like a superhero and am instantly pissed no one was around to see it. Erin would laugh and tell me I'm so far from the suave boss bitch she met. And then I would tell her this is the real me. Bookish, nerdy, a little silly, and a lot in love with her. Then she'd kiss me and call me a dork. She'd be right. The Amelia she met was suave and all that jazz, but it was somewhat of a facade to make her fall in love with me. And it worked.

Rounding the corner, I spot Chris and Simon exactly where I left them. My heart beats a little slower.

"The coast is clear. But I'd prefer to go on foot. The sound of the bikes will ricochet around the buildings, causing too much noise. We still need to keep a low profile."

"Agreed. Come on, let's go," Chris replies, already taking off at speed. There is still no sign of danger when we reach the rendezvous point. Chris motions down the street. "They came from the alley around the side of the building. We'd only just arrived."

"Then what happened?"

"We scattered, but they were suddenly coming from every direction. I was able to dodge them. I got to the end of the block and turned around, ready to fight any fucker who followed. But no one did. I saw them bundle Mack, Jordan, and another vampire into the back of a van. I tried to follow them, Amelia, but I couldn't keep up. I don't have your speed."

Laying both hands on his shoulders, I look him in the eye. "This isn't on you, Chris." It's on Mohan. Okay, I'm still not over that. "You did the right thing. You got word to us and now we're here. So stop feeling guilty." I know he wants to protest. I understand him fully, and I too would be blaming myself, regardless. "I'm going to circle the place and see if anything gives us a clue."

"We should go inside, make sure there are no vampires waiting."

I sniff. "I can't smell anyone here, but double-check."

Simon takes the lead, this time ushering Chris inside. They make a good partnership. I wonder if they'll be friends after this. Chris could use a buddy. I know he has Erin, Mack, Jordan and me, but that's two mated couples. It can't be much fun for him at times.

I take a slow, methodical walk around the entire exterior. Now and then I stop and inhale deeply. I can smell Mack. Well, a trace of her. It's old. It lingers in the air, but faintly. She's not here. Jordan's scent is missing, but that might be because I still have a link with her mate and therefore can recognize it easily.

A whiff of men's cologne makes me wince. It's strong. I've smelled that before. One of the assholes who tried to attack Erin and me in Hawaii had a lingering scent of the same brand on his skin.

It's either a coincidence or it's the same assault team. A dark voice tells me I should have killed them when I had the chance. Shaking my head, I force the noise out of my head.

I can use the cologne alongside Mack's scent. Satisfied, I can start tracing them. I head inside and retrieve Chris and Simon. As suspected, there is no one here, but Chris shows me a scrap of paper. Mack's scent is all over it, along with...Jordan's. I feel the relief wash over me. It's likely they were taken together. Clearly my ability to track scent *is* enhanced when it's the smell of a human I've turned. For once, I'm grateful for the bond.

The paper has a roughly written number scrawled on the bottom half. I'm guessing it's a phone number. Whether it's for a vampire in need or something else entirely is anyone's guess. We haven't got time to deal with it this second. Chris stows it in his jacket for later.

We move swiftly back to the bikes. I'm hyper aware of our surroundings, but we seem to be safe.

"You guys take the bikes. I can't track them with a helmet on, and like you said, I'm rather fast on my feet." I grin.

"Okay, take this," Simon utters, looking a little pink in the cheeks. I look down as he pulls a phone from his pocket. "It's untraceable. Your sister gave it to me. The scary one. She told me not to give it to you unless you, and I quote 'go off on your own like a fucking idiot.' Um...so here."

Gritting my teeth, I take the phone. "Did she look like an old hag with witchy fingers?" Simon doesn't know how to respond, which makes me laugh. "I'm kidding. I know which sister you're referring to. She's adopted. We think she's actually the daughter of Lilith, sent to earth to destroy all things beautiful." I hear Erin snort in my head, which brings a smile to my face.

Chris cackles. "You two are ridiculous."

I smile at him and wiggle my eyebrows. "I'm right though, she's the worst."

"Okay, we can dissect your overly competitive and volatile relationship with Lucille later. We have work to do. Simon, do you have another phone? It's no help if Amelia has no one to call."

"Here," he replies, handing it to Chris. "The scary sister slapped this into my palm before storming off."

I slap Chris on the back. "Let's go." The boys don their helmets and slip on the bikes. "Head east a few miles. If anyone sees you driving strangely, it'll only draw attention to you. Chris, I'll call you when I change direction or find something."

Shaking out my limbs like an athlete, I wink over my shoulder before running away. A small cloud of dust is the only evidence I was ever there. Chris and Simon rev the bikes as they follow. I tune them out and concentrate.

My mind calms as I run, following Mack's scent. I can still smell the cologne along with leather and sweat. The little piece of paper Chris found gave me more than I realized. My ability is still growing it seems. I can filter the different scents and separate them. If I lose track of Mack and Jordan, I have plenty of other clues to fall back on. Good for me, unlucky for the assholes I'm hunting.

God, I hope he's there when I find them. I hope the whole team is there. This time, I won't be so lenient.

Eighteen

ERIN

The hours have melded together in one terrifying pot of endless and death-defying travel. Lucille should have all licenses stripped away and never returned. I thought things would get better once we left the continent and all threats of the Special Forces. I thought we'd swap to bigger aircraft, or boats, or whatever. I was so wrong. Lucille has crammed us in tiny vehicles for what seems to be days now. Rationally, I know that's an exaggeration, but my thumping heart and spiked adrenaline feel like it's been days of torture. It's not like I'd die if Lucille finally lost control, but the others would. I fear for them as much as myself.

We've just landed in Singapore to the audible relief of everyone. We made the collective decision to stop here for a day before flying over to the island. Marcus continues his never-ending and enthusiastic dialogue about Asia's biggest island as my feet hit the tarmac. I could bow down and kiss the ground in sheer delight. Paula and Ricco look a little wobbly as they disembark. It wouldn't surprise me if they've been scared off air travel for the rest of their days.

Lucille jumps down from the plane with a giant smile attached to her face. I think this is the happiest I have ever seen her. "I rented us a house for a few nights."

"Aren't we heading to the island tomorrow?" Marcus asks, his eyes fixed on a guidebook.

"Yes. But it doesn't hurt to have a place to crash when we get back from wading through the jungle," Lucille replies, rolling her eyes as if Marcus's comment was the stupidest thing she's ever heard.

I clear my throat. "It could take us more than a few days, Luce."

Now she turns her rolling eyes on me. "Obviously. The house owner knows to keep the place open for us. Relax."

I want to burst out laughing. There's not a cat in hell's chance any of us are relaxing, not after we've spent so long clenching and fearing for our lives. It'll take several strong drinks and a deep tissue massage before I'm the least bit relaxed.

I send a quick check-in with Amelia. She feels me and sends her love. I've managed to stay out of her head so far. Apart from when she called Lucille the daughter of Lilith. That made me snort-chuckle. It wasn't very attractive.

I pull my pack over my arms and follow Lucille, who has become the unspoken leader of the group. A fact I am more than okay with. We round the corner of the tiny hangar and spot a large SUV idling. Before our fearless maniac gets her hands on the keys, I use my speed to zip past and whip them out of the hands of a surprised Chinese vampire. What's the protocol here? Should I bow? That's polite in Chinese culture, right? I hedge my bets, and he seems more than pleased when I lift my head back up. I make a mental note to add China to my ever-growing list of places to visit on vacation.

Lucille stands with her hands on her hips, scowling at me.

"You need a break," I say feebly before slipping behind the wheel. Of course she rides shotgun, grumbling as I pull off. This is only the second time I've driven in a foreign country and I'm not one hundred percent confident in my ability to get us there without incident, but I'd still rather risk it than let Lucille drive. Plus, Marcus, Paula, and Ricco look relieved for the first time in many, *many* hours.

We pull up to a McMansion ten minutes later. Could she have picked a more conspicuous place to stay?

"Luce this…it's not very low key."

"Pfft. We've been living in a concrete box. I need a hot bath and silk sheets and light. Screw low key. Anyway, we're surrounded by a massive wall and the security system is top-notch, plus we have you. I'm not worried."

That's that then, I guess. Although I have to agree, the thought of soaking in a tub sounds heavenly.

The house is all sleek lines and chrome. A little disappointing, to be honest. It's so sterile. For a country as rich in history as Singapore, I'd have thought the place would have more character.

Lucille drops her pack by the huge entry door. She wheels 'round, hands on hips again. "It's owned by Ronald Merland. He's an oil baron."

"American?" Ricco asks.

"Obviously. Texan. I think this is his play pad, away from the wife." Lucille grins.

Ugh, the thought makes me cringe. At least I know why the place holds no characteristics of its heritage.

"I hope the place has been hosed down," Marcus mumbles, screwing up his nose as he looks around.

Lucille claps, which reverberates around the colossal atrium. "Grab a room and then meet back down here. I've got a surprise for you all."

I'm too beat to care. Stumbling up the glass steps, I throw myself on the first bed I see, praying it isn't the master suite. I'm almost asleep when I get dragged off the bed by my feet. *Lucille.* My patience is wearing thin. I'm starting to see why she and Amelia fight so much.

"I need rest, Luce."

"You can rest when you're old. Downstairs."

It would be wrong to jump into her mind and knock her out, wouldn't it? *Sigh.* Yeah, it would, dammit. Everyone else looks as moody as me as they stand in the living room. God, I want to whine and stamp my feet.

Lucille stands tall and imposing. "Tomorrow is going to be tough. Much tougher than the past few days. We've got one hell of a search on our hands in unfamiliar territory." *Okay, Bear Grylls.* "When we do find the hut, we have no idea what we'll come across. It could be nothing, or it could be something we have to guard ourselves against."

"This is a fab pep talk," I mumble.

"It's reality Erin. So, before we all part for the night, I've organized a little something. No alcohol, which hurts my heart a little." She chuckles. "I could skull several bottles of wine right now. But no. I have bottles of fresh Red waiting for you in the kitchen. And...a karaoke machine."

A what now? "I'm sorry." I chuckle. "Did you say karaoke?"

Lucille nods enthusiastically. "I did. We're going to load up on Red and then belt some songs out. We're all far too tense."

"I definitely need booze," Ricco replies.

Who is this woman? Snarky uptight Lucille wants to do karaoke! I've got to get this on camera. Amelia is going to freak. Maybe I should see if she wants to watch? No, this is not the time to be distracting her. I'm definitely recording it.

"You first, then Luce. Show us how it's done," Paula shouts.

Without hesitation, she taps in a song to the machine and waits for the music to blare through the house speaker system. Lucille's rendition of "I Wanna Dance With Somebody" is really fucking impressive. I can't believe this is the first time I'm witnessing her like this. The earlier fatigue that surrounded the group seems to flitter away with every note. Paula grabs Ricco's hand and they start dancing. Laughter rings out as Ricco twirls her around.

Marcus wastes no time and jumps up to the mic once Lucille is finished. Is this a Loch thing? Are they all secretly karaoke nuts? Does Amelia do this with them? Oh my god, I bet she does. I bet this is what they do when they have "family meetings." I'm usually in attendance, but there have been a handful of times I couldn't make it, and Amelia was suspiciously okay with it. I bet she's got a small dark corner of her brain walled off from me that's full of karaoke night madness with the family.

Meat Loaf's "I'd Do Anything for Love" echoes around the room. And, of course, Marcus is a phenomenal singer. I'm praying the change from human to mega vampire has drastically improved my singing voice.

It has not.

Now, I'm not tone deaf but after following the Loch siblings I sound like a dying cat. Still, I have to admit it is fun belting out my favorite Celine Dion song. It takes me back to my teenage years, dancing and jumping on my bed with a hairbrush. It was lonely as an only child; I had to entertain myself somehow.

We take turns singing a few more songs before Paula announces she needs to sleep because she's close to face planting the floor. I stay behind to help Lucille clear up the now empty bottles of Red.

"That was a lot of fun," I say. She was right. We needed to let off some steam.

"Of course it was. Who doesn't like karaoke?"

I study her for a bit as we wipe down the counter in the kitchen. "Why don't we get to see this side of you, Luce?"

I'm genuinely curious. Lucille makes sure she comes across as acidic most of the time. Only a few people get to see her soft center. She remains silent for a few moments, making me worry I've upset her.

"I don't find it easy opening up to many people. It's not easy growing up in the middle of seven other kids. I guess I learned young that my sharp tongue and kick ass moves garnered more attention."

"I'm sure it was tough for you all."

"Marcus and Laurence are the eldest. They get instant older sibling privileges. Maria, Aliah, and Lucas are the fun ones. Bratty but the life and soul of the party."

"And Amelia?"

She suddenly turns to me. "If you repeat this to her, I'll disembowel you!"

"Noted."

She squints her eyes at me, assessing if I'm being truthful. I clearly pass. "I always looked up to Amelia. She was quiet like me. I know, I know," she says, waving her hand in dismissal of the obvious rebuttal I was about to make. The Lucille I know is anything but quiet. "You all see me as this loudmouth who causes trouble. But believe it or not, I wasn't always like that. Sure, I was intense. I still am. But when I was a kid, I found it difficult to open up. Amelia was always so...stoic. Also, a bit of a loner. She preferred her books to her annoying baby sister."

I'm picking up what she's putting down. "So you started fights with her to hang out?"

She shrugs. "Pretty much. Weirdly, I felt it brought us closer together. Mother would dispute that, especially when she had to drag us apart. But...and I stick by this. Our fighting, my goading, it helped Amelia let out some of her feelings. It helped me bond with her. Okay, probably not in a super healthy way, but still."

My heart breaks a little for her. "Do you feel uncomfortable acting like this," gesturing to the karaoke machine, "in front of Amelia?"

Another shrug. "We've gotten closer over the past couple of years. I think you have a lot to do with that. She doesn't rise to the bait anymore, and...well, I like you, Erin.

I think we get on, and that's bridged another gap between me and Amelia."

I hop onto the counter. "You know, I think your bitching and moaning are good for her!"

Lucille's eyebrows get lost in her raven hair. "You're the first person to think so." She laughs.

"It's true," I reply. "Amelia is a loner. Of course, she's my mate, and we're usually stuck at the hip, but she easily gets lost in her own thoughts. These past few weeks have been really fucking hard on us. Amelia has been finding all the changes difficult to process. It's not been easy getting her to open up. I've done my fair share of overthinking, I know. But I'm nowhere near as hard on myself as your sister is on herself. The thing is Luce. It wasn't me that got her to re-evaluate her feelings, it was you. By beating the crap out of each other in the bunker."

Lucille's cheeks tinge red. "I knew she was looking for a fight, is all."

"No, you knew what your sister needed to help her process all the harsh changes she was struggling to digest. You're her closest sibling, by far."

"Marcus and Amelia—"

"Don't have the same bond as you. When shit hits the fan, it's you she comes to. It's you she's trusted to take care of me. We both know she wouldn't have let Marcus do this alone. You are her right hand. And I know she would love to see this other side of you. Because she has the same playfulness. You just have to trust in each other."

"Jesus, I thought you were a bartender?"

I laugh. "Aren't bartenders cheap shrinks?" I wink. "I'm just saying you don't have to keep your walls up so much."

She huffs. "I'm going to hug you now, but don't make a big deal about it." I roll my lips to stop myself from laughing and accept her hug. "I'll think about it, okay? But not until we've finished here. I need to keep my boss bitch wall up in that jungle. I promised to keep you safe, and I intend to honor my word. So y'all will just have to put up with me scowling for a little while longer."

Laughing, I hop down and pat her on the shoulder. "I don't want you to change completely, Luce. It would be weird if you didn't insult people on a regular basis."

"I'll remember you said that." She grins.

Nineteen

AMELIA

Bumfuck nowhere, Utah. That's where my nose has led us. Thankfully, the majority of our travels saw little human existence. I didn't have to worry about being spotted running at an impossible speed. I'm physically exhausted. My mind wants to continue searching, but my body is on the verge of collapse. Am I in a state of delirium and Mack's scent is a figment of my imagination? I want to find our friends so desperately. I'm scared I've made the trail up in my head. I mean, what the hell is in Utah? Gold Hill, Utah. Let me tell you. Nothing! Nothing apart from desolate buildings and dirt. It's a ghost town.

Simon and Chris are circling the area on foot while I rest. They did an admirable job keeping up. Although I had to stop now and then to send new coordinates when the scent changed direction suddenly. Every muscle is screaming at me to stop and lie down for the next ten years. A gentle breeze has me turn my head. Cologne. And it's fresh. Those fuckers are here somewhere. I can feel it.

"There's nothing obvious," Chris whispers.

"They're here," I say dangerously. In my current state of mind, I'm ready to rip the bastards limb from limb.

"You need to rest, Amelia." I start to protest, but Chris stops me with a gentle squeeze on my shoulder. "We will need all our strength. We also need time to locate them and strategize."

My head drops to my chest, and I let out a long, tired sigh. "You're right. I can't go much longer."

"You've literally run from LA to Utah, Amelia. I can't believe you're still standing," Simon comments, crouching down by my legs. "Well, you know what I mean." He smiles. I didn't even notice I'd sunk to the floor. Clearly my legs have stopped working all together.

Christopher holds his hand out to me. "There's an abandoned ranch a few miles south. Let's hole up there for the night and assess things in the morning."

Nodding, I take the proffered help, groaning as I stand. Taking one last look around, I follow Simon and Chris to the bikes. I've never been more grateful to ride pillion. My body practically falls onto Chris as I hold on. Closing my eyes, I think of Erin, wondering where she is. We've both kept our distance, so to speak. Only a quick "I love you" and "I'm okay." Distraction can be deadly, and it's already hard enough being apart.

I'd give anything to have her in my arms. I picture her beautiful gold hair and how it tickles me in the face every night. Erin's soft features as she sleeps. I can't bring myself to think of her body because that's just self-torture, so I concentrate on her face. The smile she gives me every morning, or the fire that blazes in her eyes when I do or say something to piss her off. How she stands up to my family in all her small yet mighty glory. How my family is a little afraid of her. That makes me smile. Even before she became a formidable vampire, her sassy little ass never backed down from the Lochs, and they loved her more for it.

My memories last until Chris pulls the bike over to a well-worn ranch house. The roof's still intact, so that's a bonus. Maybe there will be a couple of old beds to rest on. My back doesn't like the idea of laying on a hard floor.

It smells of damp and sadness inside. The house is furnished, but there is a layer of thick dust on every surface. I wonder who lived here and why they had to leave? I'm sure at one point, love and laugher lived within these walls.

"Drink this, Amelia." I turn to Simon, who is holding out a bottle of Red. Taking it, I drain it in seconds. Erin's blood still courses through my veins, giving me a boost, but I know I need a top up. "Now sleep. There's a bedroom down the hall. Chris and I will take turns on lookout."

"Are you sure?"

I'm not the only one who needs rest. Chris and Simon may have been on bikes, but they've not stopped either.

"Go. We'll wake you in a few hours," Chris replies.

Aware my legs are seconds from buckling, I stumble down the hall. The room is pleasant, but it still feels weird laying in someone else's bed. I let my mind wander to the events of the day. It took us nearly fifteen hours to get here. There were a few stops and readjustments as we went. I'm still amazed I can smell Mack. It is possible that the link we share enables me to dial into her somehow. But then again, I can also smell the soldier's cologne, too. The only bond we share is a violent one. My warrior perks up. Vivid memories of that night in Hawaii flood my mind. And then

I understand. *She* has made that bond with him. With all the soldiers.

Lucille told me that this "other" side of me is still *me*. We are one, and I agree. To a point. I know I had to accept it to be the person Erin needed. However, after some contemplation, I believe it's a little more complex than that. There is a reason I felt out of control when I changed. Why this new side of me felt foreign. Because it was, *it is*. I've not voiced these thoughts because they might sound a little farfetched, but I think my warrior and Erin's queen *are* separate entities that have bonded with our souls. We cohabitate, drawing power from them. I don't think it's evolution. I think it's...well, a kind of magic.

It sounds nuts, I know, but my warrior has her own mind. I created the bond with Mack when I turned her. I believe I draw the ability to help humans from my warrior, however I think she can make separate bonds. But hers are with those who have threatened us.

My body sinks heavier into the bed as I ponder. I feel a wave of pride wash over me as I work through my thoughts. Is my warrior proud of me for working it out?

Yup, I definitely sound cuckoo. I need to sleep.

Vivid dreams plague me all night until I wake with a start. My fangs descend and I breathe hard. I'm a bundle of confusion as I try to recall what I saw. For some reason, I have Whitney Houston and Meat Loaf playing on a loop in my head.

Rolling off the bed, I stretch and try to wake my body up. As predicted, it hurts. Everywhere. But underneath the ache is an energy that is becoming more present as I focus on it. I feel venom soak my fangs. What the hell is going on?

Suddenly my back is ramrod straight and my head snaps back. Mack. I can see her. I've no idea how this is possible, but it's happening. They've tied her hands up above her head. She's bleeding in several spots on her face. Although she looks unconscious, I know she is awake, calling out to me.

As quickly as it came, the vision ends and I crumble to the floor, panting. The sound of my fall alerts Chris and Simon, who burst through the door. I look up and their eyes widen. I guess it's the sight of my fangs. Breathing deep,

I focus on calming down. After a few seconds, my fangs recede. Although I feel wobbly, I stand.

"Mack is close," I rasp. "I saw her."

"How?" Chris asks, coming to my side and wrapping his arm around my waist. He maneuvers me to the bed so I can sit.

"I don't know how. But she's here."

"Is she injured?" Simon asks.

"A few cuts to the face."

Chris paces. "Did you see anyone else?"

"No, just Mack. She's somewhere dark. I couldn't see much."

"Okay. This is good," Chris says, more to himself than to Simon and me. "It must mean the link you share is getting stronger. We can use that."

"Amelia needs more rest. Look at her," Simon states. "She's as white as a sheet."

"No," I protest. "No more rest. If we have any Red, I'll take that, but we go now. I'm not letting our friends spend another minute in that hellhole."

"She's right, Simon. No more waiting."

He doesn't seem happy, but he backs down. "Fine. Do you want to head back to Gold Hill?"

I shake my head. "She's a little outside Gold Hill."

Chris brings up a map on his burner. "Here," he says after several minutes. "There's an old mine a few miles away. It's secluded. Ideal place to hold a few vampires prisoner."

"We can't ride the bikes. They'll know we're coming from miles away," Simon says, studying Chris's phone.

"Then we run."

Chris chuckles. "Neither of us can run at your pace, Amelia."

"I know, so let's get going. I'll run ahead and check the area out."

Simon holds up his finger and leaves the room. He's back within seconds and holding another bottle of Red. "Have a drink first."

"Thanks, Mom," I say, taking the bottle. Simon blushes. "Oh my god! My mom had you promise to feed me Red, didn't she?"

"Hey," Simon protests. "You Lochs are like seven feet tall, and Momma Loch is scary as hell. There was no way I was going to argue with her."

Laughter bubbles up and out. "She is scary as hell."

"Right, so drink up." Simon grins.

Full to the brim with Red, I feel reinvigorated. We pack our things and leave the ranch house. I still find it rather sad it's being left to rot.

"Meet me here," I say, pointing to a patch of land that should provide us with cover.

Chris hugs me. "Good luck and be safe."

They set off running, leaving me alone for a few moments. "Are you ready for this?" I say out loud. My warrior beats her chest. She's ready. I draw all the energy I can from her. Power envelopes me and my blue light shimmers over my skin. I feel Erin's presence momentarily, and it boosts me further.

Turning on my heel, I propel myself forward. I pass Chris and Simon in seconds. The world rushes by in a blur, but I'm too focused on my target to pay much attention. A small dust cloud kicks up as I skid to a stop. The old mine is a few hundred yards away. My eyes scan feverishly for signs of life. One solitary guard is at the shaft entrance. There will be more inside, but I'm not worried. I could take them all out myself, but I won't deny Simon and Chris. They've earned the right to storm the castle. I crouch down, waiting and watching until I hear the boys arrive. They're a little sweaty, but no worse for wear.

"Nice jog?" I quip.

"Delightful," Chris murmurs.

"There's just one guy so far," I say, gesturing to the soldier now taking a leak up a wooden post.

"There will be more inside," Simon says.

"I'm betting it will be an entire team of Special Forces." I can smell that fucking cologne. "I'll take out numb nuts over there. Don't move until I tell you to."

The poor bastard hasn't even finished zipping himself up when I arrive by his side. His hands fumble and his eyes grow wide in panic. I give him a snide grin before knocking him out. My warrior cries for more. She wants this asshole's head on a platter, but I can't let that happen. I won't be a monster.

After depositing the soldier's body behind a pile of rocks, I wave for Chris and Simon to join me. Simon goes straight for the soldier, binding his hands with plastic ties. He slaps a piece of tape over the guy's mouth and then stands back to survey his work. "You're not going anywhere, asswipe."

"We stay silent," I whisper. "No heroics. Understand?" They both nod. "I'll go first. When we find Mack and Jordan, you help them get free. I'll deal with the team."

It's go-time.

Twenty

ERIN

My hair is in a tight bun, and I'm covered in an entire can of bug spray. Okay, maybe two. Stupidly, I asked Marcus about the kinds of bugs we might encounter. He went into great detail, which made my skin crawl. Hence the overuse of poisonous chemicals now soaking into my skin and clothes.

With the lightweight pack strapped to my back, I stand silently, waiting for Lucille to finish talking with the boat captain we've hired to take us to the island. As promised, Lucille is back to her usual abrasive self. She's all work now. Last night's entertainment might as well have happened years ago. There is no joviality as we ready ourselves for the days ahead. Paula and Ricco stand next to me, holding hands. Marcus is repacking his bag for the tenth time. We're all pleased that the mode of transport changed from air to sea. Well, maybe not Lucille. But Paula staunchly refused to get on another plane, so she didn't have much choice. She's still sour about it.

"He's ready to go," Lucille shouts. We quick march over and climb aboard. There are commercial ferries, but we'd stick out like sore thumbs with our gear. None of us look like tourists. I'm not a huge fan of boats, but I'll suck it up. This is the last leg of the journey before we'll be on foot. I should enjoy the rest while I can.

"We'll arrive in about ten hours," Lucille announces once we've made ourselves comfortable in the small living area. There's a kitchenette, sofa and built-in table. Every surface has a trinket on it. The captain must live onboard permanently.

"What's the plan after that?" Ricco asks.

Lucille smiles. "We take a light aircraft from Kuching to Mulu Airport." There's a collective groan. "I knew you'd like that."

I can see Paula weighing up the urge to argue or accept her fate. She sighs and slumps her shoulders. Lucille wins.

"From there, we can use the park trails to make it to the rocks. After that, it's down to you, Erin," Marcus says.

Thanks for the reminder.

I smile and nod. I've said all I have to say on the matter. We'll either find something helpful or not. I can't keep worrying about it. My senses prickle as I sit there listening to the others chat. Amelia is summoning her energy, which makes my heart rate spike. Does that mean she's found Mack and Jordan? I do the only thing I can think of to help and push more of my energy her way. A low hum remains in my chest and my fingertips buzz. I'm still getting used to these kinds of things happening.

After a while, the hum dissipates, leaving me hollow. I so desperately want to know what's happening. Closing my eyes, I reach out to Jordan. I gasp as I feel her. Instead of everlasting blackness, I see a blur of light. Her mind is dull, which I'm guessing means she's still under the influence of drugs, but not to the level that is shutting down her mind.

Jordan?

No answer, but I feel her presence. She wants to talk to me, but she is still too intoxicated.

"Erin?" Lucille's sharp voice pulls me from my mind. "Erin, talk to me."

My hands tightly grip my chest, and my breathing becomes labored. "She found them," I sob. "Amelia found them."

The second I focus on my wife, pain replaces my overwhelming relief. She's hurt. Oh, god. I stumble to my feet and head for the cabin door. I have to get off this boat. I have to get to Amelia.

"Erin, stop!" Lucille is gripping my shoulders, trying to pull me back. A well of anger rises. I spin on my feet and push her away. She lands on the other side of the cabin with a bang. Several ornaments fall to the deck.

"Erin, calm down," Marcus says in a steady tone. "Talk to us."

"I have to get to Amelia."

Lucille is back on her feet in seconds. Her face snarls in a sadistic grin. "You're not going anywhere."

Before I know what's happening, she has me in a full body grip. My fangs descend instinctually, and I battle with all my strength to free myself of her grip. There's a reason Amelia chooses her sister as a sparring partner. Lucille is solid muscle under that tall frame. She's not necessarily stronger than me, but her years of martial arts training have me pinned to the ground before I can blink.

"Calm the fuck down," she hisses.

"Let me go!" I roar. Gold threads curl around my fists.

"No. Amelia wouldn't want this," she growls, tightening her grip on me. "She needs you to stay on course, Erin."

"She's hurt, Lucille. I have to go to her!"

"Is she dead?"

The question has me sucking in a lungful of air. "No," I stutter.

"Then we carry on. This is too important, Erin."

Nothing is more important than my mate. Nothing!

"I understand. Believe me, I do. If this were Trent, I'd be acting just the same. But you have to find it within yourself to fight your instincts. Amelia will recover. She's found Mack and Jordan. Now you have to fulfill your part of this. Please Erin, I'm begging you."

To my surprise, Lucille loosens her hold and shuffles away. She sits back on her legs and simply looks at me. Her eyes pleading. I'm lying on the floor breathing heavily.

"I..." I'm lost for words. I know Lucille is right. Amelia would want me to carry on.

Closing my eyes, I focus on Amelia. She's unconscious. She's in pain, but she's alive.

Amelia?

Nothing. I scour the depths of her mind until I find her blue light. Her mind is protecting itself, allowing Amelia to heal.

Amelia, my love, I'm here. I'm with you.

Silence.

Panic claws at my chest. All I need is to hear her voice, but my pleas go unanswered. Coating her light in my love, I pull back. Without thinking, I search for Chris. He answers me in seconds.

She's Okay Erin. I've got her. We found Jordan and Mack. Plus a few more vampires. We dealt with the soldiers.

What the hell happened?

Amelia took a few dozen rounds to the chest.

A few dozen rounds? She's been shot multiple times? Oh god I want to hurl.

She's safe, Erin, I swear it.

Where are you?

Utah.

Huh, I wasn't expecting that.

We'll head to the bunker as soon as Amelia is able.

Swallowing hard, I make a decision that I am sure will haunt me for the rest of my life.

Okay. Take care of her.

My soul is screaming for me to choose her. Choose to go home and hold her close. I feel as if I am betraying our very existence by staying here.

Severing our connection, I keep my eyes closed for a few seconds longer, willing the tears I feel to remain unshed. All eyes are on me the second I sit up.

"We continue on."

The rest of the trip is spent in silence. I have no energy to spare answering questions and thankfully, my team respects my need for space. I try to reach Amelia every half an hour, but nothing. I can only conclude her injuries are severe enough that her body needs longer to heal.

We only tested the theory once. I remember when Amelia stabbed herself in the abdomen to prove herself right. I could have throttled her. I'm pretty sure her mother did. Based on that one test, and the fact I got shot in the heart and survived, we concluded that both of us are invincible. What if we were wrong? What if Amelia's injuries are too much for her to come back from?

Erin.

It's a whisper of a sound, but I hear it.

Erin, my love.

Amelia? Warmth blossoms through my cells. My soul basks in it. *Oh, my darling.*

Those unshed tears are now cascading down my cheeks. Paula rushes to my side with concern. I smile at her brightly. "Amelia is awake."

I'm okay, my love. Sore, but okay.

I'm sorry I didn't come to you.

The guilt is already eating me alive.

You did the right thing. We need to finish this, honey.

I tell her how much I love her before disengaging to let her rest. Paula is still by my side. Ricco sits opposite with Marcus. Lucille stands guarding the door like she doesn't trust I'm not going to make another run for it.

"She's okay," I say to everyone. "I'm sorry about earlier." I direct this to Lucille.

Lucille winks. "As long as you're good now, we can forget it. Plus, it got the adrenaline pumping. We'll be docking soon and heading straight to the plane."

It's a herculean task, putting Amelia to the back of my mind, but I do it. There's no way in hell I'll be able to do what's needed if I'm constantly thinking of her. The fact I even have those thoughts in my head makes my stomach churn and the guilt builds up a little more. But what choice do I have?

We dock and disembark. The humidity slaps me in the face instantly. I can already feel my hair trying to frizz. The journey to the airfield takes twenty minutes by car. The air conditioning is delightful, and I'm genuinely upset about leaving the rental for a tiny sweatbox. We'll be in the air less than two hours, but with Lucille at the helm it'll feel a hell of a lot longer.

The aircraft is as small as expected. I settle into a meditation as soon as I'm in my seat. My neurons are firing on all cylinders, so I need to calm down. Locking onto the voice that called me in my dreams isn't going to be easy. It'll take all my concentration, and maybe a few prayers to the universe for some guidance. Once again, it's time to switch off Erin and pull forward the Salvator Regina. Everything in my mind washes away as I focus intently on the hut. I can see it so clearly. I want whoever or whatever has been calling me to know I am close.

The landing is atrocious, and I vow to never get in a vehicle Lucille is driving ever again. I'll walk home if necessary. The glint in her eye and wolfish grin makes me think she's flown like an asshole just for kicks. Let's see how funny it is when I regurgitate Red all over her.

Marcus suddenly comes to life the second we step foot on solid ground. His map comes out, and he's already walking off. Paula shrugs her shoulders and follows him. Ricco chuckles, picks up their rucksacks, and jogs after them to catch up.

The energy around me changes as I move on. Marcus is yammering away at anyone who will listen about the history of the land. Lucille remains silent, but I feel her eyes on me now and then. Can she sense something is happening to me?

The jungle feels suffocating when I step into the tree line. The birdsong is just as loud as in my dreams. There is no wind, though. No sound of my name rustling through the trees. But there is a presence. An energy that prickles my senses.

We walk for hours, stopping to rehydrate now and then. There is little talk. Even Marcus has fallen quiet. The weight of our expedition hangs heavy on our shoulders. The day is getting away from us. According to the map, we are only an hour's walk from the outpost where we will sleep for the night. I can see the jagged rocks from my dream in the far distance now.

I'm so lost in my thoughts I don't see Ricco stop in front of me and I plow right into him.

"Crap, I'm sorry," I say, although it's me on my ass.

Ricco looks at me and then scratches his head. "Um…Erin, look at your hands."

Looking down, I see what's got him staring at me. The gold threads are back. I'm starting to feel like a goddamn Christmas light display. Jumping back to my feet, I hold both hands out in front of me. The group is watching with palpable anticipation. I forget that my aura usually only shows when I'm with Amelia. Usually in the middle of an orgasm. So this is different. The only other time people have witnessed it was when Amelia and I fought Noah. And none of those people are here now, which is why Marcus, Lucille, Ricco, and Paula are staring at me. By the look on their faces, it must seem like I'm the second coming, I guess.

My hands glow brighter and then the threads snake away from my body. They veer off our chosen path and to the left.

"This way," I whisper.

Twenty-One

AMELIA

Everything hurts. My fucking insides are on fire. I can't believe that asshole emptied a clip into me. How didn't I notice him? If I'd spotted him a second sooner, I wouldn't be on the floor outside an abandoned mine half bleeding to death and he wouldn't be...

My god, what have I done?

Everything went according to plan. We followed the electric lamps down the shaft until we found the room where Jordan, Mack, and several other vampires were being held. I incapacitated the soldiers easily. They didn't see me coming. Why didn't I make sure I'd gotten *him*? I'd followed his scent for nearly a thousand miles and yet I didn't take a second to check. All I know is my focus shifted to Mack and Jordan when the last soldier fell unconscious. Jordan was curled up in a ball at the far end of the room, shivering. Her body battered and bruised. A bucket of water and a towel lay discarded next to her. The fuckers had waterboarded the poor girl.

Mack was semi-conscious, only able to make garbled sounds through a clearly broken jaw. As for the others, they were in different states. Some wide-eyed and shaking, others unresponsive.

I ran to Jordan and picked her up, and that's when I felt the first sting of a bullet pierce my back. I dropped her and fell to my knees, but I wasn't down for long. I spun around, ready to face the threat. My fangs came out and my warrior raged inside.

He was hiding in the shadows of the room. The soldier with the cologne. The second he saw my teeth, he pulled the trigger, over and over. I felt every shot. I remember falling to the ground, my head hitting stone.

I didn't black out. I heard Chris scream my name and then felt a weight press me down harder. That scent was in my nose again, but so much stronger. He'd climbed on my back. I felt the barrel of the gun bury in my hair. My warrior roared inside, pulling every ounce of strength I had left.

I managed to turn around until I faced him. The soldier's eyes whipped to my teeth. He tried to reposition his gun, but my hand found his throat. I squeezed and squeezed until I heard a snap. His vacant eyes stared at me until I finally broke out of the red haze which had overtaken me. I'd killed him.

Simon was the one to drag his body off me and then carry me outside. Mack and Jordan lay close by. Chris was tending to them while a couple of the other vampires helped each other. My shock must have worn off because that's when the inferno of pain started.

I remember ripping my shirt off and looking at my abdomen. There was a sea of crimson pouring out. My t-shirt wasn't enough to help stem the blood flow. I honestly thought I was going to die, regardless of the fact I believed myself invincible.

The wounds twinged painfully. The bullets worked their way out of my body, but I only saw black after that as the pain became too much. That is until I heard her. Erin. She called to me in the darkness, beckoning me to return. Her golden light wrapped itself around me, keeping me safe.

I don't know how long it took me, but eventually I called to her, and my heart beat a little harder when I heard her sweet voice.

Amelia?

Just my name from her lips was a salve to my broken body. I tried to reassure her. The selfish part of me wanted her to come to me. But I couldn't face her. Not after what I'd done. Erin always said she believed I wouldn't become what I feared. That I wasn't a monster. How the hell do I tell her she was wrong? I'm a murderer.

My body is healing, slowly. Mack and Jordan are both awake now. Jordan can speak a little. Not enough to tell us what's happened to them since being here. Our priority is getting them back to the safety of the bunker, but I'm not sure I can walk yet.

Chris kneels by my side, checking the bullet holes. They've stopped bleeding, and the skin is knitting back together.

"We need to get you and the rest of them some medical attention. I'm going to call Mohan with the burner. We need help, and we've been out here far too long already."

I've no idea what the time is or how long ago we entered the mine, and I'm more than happy to receive some backup. Our task is done. We've found the kidnapped vampires. Now I'm quite happy to hand over the reins to someone else.

"Here, drink this," Simon murmurs as he gently lifts my head. "It's the last of our Red, but you need it to help with the healing."

I try to turn my lips away from the bottle. I don't deserve it. I'd rather one of the other injured vampires receive it, but Simon is hard-headed and doesn't give up until I've finished it all.

Christopher rushes back over to me the second he disconnects the call. "Mohan is sending the cavalry. I told him to get here as fast as possible. We don't know what these guys were instructed to do. For all we know, they've missed a check-in and now half the US Army is on its way."

"We have to move," I gasp. The pain is still intolerable. "We're sitting ducks out here."

Simon gets to his feet. "The ranch house. It's the only place with shelter."

"How the hell are we going to move everyone?" Chris asks.

My breaths are shallow as I try to stand. *Motherfucker!* "All those who can walk need to help those who can't. Grab whatever supplies the soldiers kept in the mine that will help. We'll crawl if we have to, but we need to move."

No sooner have the words left my lips than Chris and Simon are directing people to get up and help. Summoning my warrior, I almost beg her to help me stand strong. Mack needs to be carried, and there's no way Jordan can do it. If we are attacked, I'll do my best to throw a protective shield around us, but I'm not confident it will last. That's why we have to leave now.

I stagger over to Mack, who looks terrible. Her eyes are shining with tears and pain.

"I'm sorry," I whisper before taking her into my arms. She howls through her swollen face. I've never heard a person make such a noise.

My body is angry with me, but I ignore it, focusing on my muscles and moving forward. I don't look back as I walk in the direction of the ranch house. If I look back, I'll falter because back there is the truth of who I am. I took a man's life with the tightening of my hand. He's probably a husband and father. I'll have to live with the destruction I've caused to his family for eternity. I guess that will be my penance.

"I've updated Mohan and told him we're heading to the house. I'm guessing they'll intercept us before we get there."

"I hope so."

I can see the house in the distance, but my attention is on the helicopter blades I hear getting closer. I've never been a great lover of praying, but I'll do it now. I'll pray to every deity a thousand times over if they help us get home. If they make sure those helicopters are here to take us to safety.

Stopping, I place Mack as gently as possible on the ground. Everyone stops and turns toward the ever-growing noise. I focus my gaze, willing my eyes to stay sharp. There are no military markings, but that doesn't mean the birds are friendly.

"Get behind me," I shout.

No one argues. They move as fast as their injuries will allow. My energy is seriously low, but I have to create a shield. Digging deep, I summon the last vestiges of my power to the surface of my skin. The last time I did this was to protect Erin from Noah. Erin isn't here, but the memory of that day is. I can still recall the feelings I had when Erin was threatened. I need to feel that way again to protect these people.

It's working. I feel the air ripple as the shield slowly descends. My eyes are closed in concentration, but I force myself to open them. The choppers land a few hundred feet away. Dust whirls around us in a choking cloud. Grit blasts into my eyes, but I still keep them trained on the door of the helicopter. The shield finally surrounds us entirely, cutting off the thick air. Figures emerge one by one, and I know that if they are soldiers, we are done for. My energy is close to zero, and I can feel myself slipping. The shield flickers as I do everything possible to keep it up.

"They're Mohan's guys," Chris cheers. It's the last thing I hear before collapsing to the ground in a heap.

Water splashing on my face brings me back around. I'm already loaded on the helicopter with an IV of Red strapped to my arm. Simon is sitting next to me, talking to a vampire Mohan sent. I can't make out what they're saying over the noise of the engines and blades.

The takeoff makes my stomach churn. I'm not a fan of this kind of flying. It reminds me of Lucille's piloting. It's a harrowing experience. I hope Erin hasn't had the displeasure. Surely, they would have hired a pilot, right?

Erin. My sweet soulmate who only sees the best in me.

Now that we're out of immediate danger, my mind is playing the events of the day on a loop. I'm going to have to retell the story over and over again to Mohan, the council, my parents, and Erin. They'll all know what I'm capable of. My god, what if Mother and Father keep me away from Valentine? Would I blame them?

Clearly, I'm not going to go around murdering people. I know that. It's when the anger takes over. When the red haze blinds me to my rage and I'm no longer in control. That's when I'm a liability to the people I love. Jesus, what if Chris or Simon had tried to intervene? Would I have been able to distinguish between friend and foe?

"Sleep Amelia." Simon's kind face peers down. I blink but can't find it in me to smile, so I close my eyes. The soldier's twisted face greets me the second my lids shut. He wanted me dead so badly. I disgusted and scared him enough that he wanted to snuff my life out. Is that a good enough reason to have snapped his neck? No, I could have rendered him unconscious just like the others, so what made that situation different?

His hate. I couldn't risk him living and hunting my family down. Is *that* a good enough reason? Will that be acceptable for my family to still see me as the daughter and sister they've come to know and love? Is it enough of an excuse that my wife won't see a murderer? Is it enough of a reason that I won't look in the mirror and see his dead eyes staring back at me every day?

Will that one act undo all the good I've put into this world?

I've met many Fallen who have felt the weight of their actions when they weren't in their right mind. I've seen what it can do to a person's soul. It strips them of something they can never get back. No matter how many times they are told it wasn't their fault, the guilt still plagues them. As I am positive it will me. I am them; I have fractured a part of myself that can never be fixed.

Twenty-Two

ERIN

The more we walk, the easier it is to recognize my surroundings. Every tree is familiar. Even the birdsong is a pattern I know. I listen for my name on the wind, but it is absent. We've followed my light for close to half an hour in silence. Lucille has been a constant presence next to me. I can feel her guard up. She's ready to fight.

There is nothing threatening about the energy around us, though. In fact, it's almost warm, like a mother's hug. We are being welcomed with open arms. It gives me hope that whatever is about to happen will give us the strength and knowledge to emerge victorious against the president.

The sound of a fire crackling makes me smile. We're so close now. I just hope we won't find the hut empty like in my dream. I'm not sure any of us have the patience or energy to go searching for the occupant. I'm not sure I am strong enough to keep Amelia at bay much longer.

As we break through dense undergrowth, the golden threads dim and eventually vanish. Stopping, I turn to the rest of the group. "We're here."

"Let me go first," Lucille says in a stoney voice. She's all business, and I know better than to argue. With a nod, I stand aside and let her step past me, through the last barrier of trees and into the clearing. A few moments pass and I'm about to call to her. But then she speaks. "It's safe."

Blowing a steady breath out, I step into the clearing and survey the scene. The hut is exactly as I remember it. There's even a pot hanging over the fire. But unlike my dream, the hut's owner is sitting on a stool by the fire, smiling at me.

"Regina, it's so good to finally meet you," she says warmly. Her accent is similar to Spanish, but it carries...something older in the tones. Something long forgotten.

The woman looks to be in her eighties. She has short white hair in tight curls. Her skin is weathered by the sun.

Her brown eyes sparkle and her smile is wide. I can see she has crooked teeth and possibly arthritic hands. A simple hemp dress covers her frail body.

Speak Erin!

"Hello." Well, that was less than impressive.

"Please come and sit down. You all must be hungry." She addresses the entire group, but her gaze never leaves me. It's a gaze that see's through to my soul but is not unnerving. "Sit, sit." She gestures.

Once everyone is seated, she slowly stands up and starts scooping up some sort of stew into small handmade bowls. I can feel everyone's eyes on me as she hands the food out. They're looking for reassurance it's safe to eat. I nod and then laugh when Ricco and Marcus practically inhale the food. We've had plenty of Red and snacks to keep us going, but there is something about the stew that smells amazing and sets my mouth watering.

She sits back down and turns her attention to me again. "My name is Balam."

"E-erin."

She bows her head slightly. "It is a beautiful name."

I sit silently, studying her. She eyes me back with a silent challenge. She wants to see if I can work it out. I think I have. There is a reason she is so familiar to me. I have a theory, and if it's correct, we are sitting in the presence of an ancient vampire. The vampire who preceded me as the Salvator Regina. I have to test her.

Pushing my aura out, I envelop her in my light. My breath catches when she absorbs it, with a wink, no less. I was right.

Standing, I move to her and drop to both knees. "It's an honor to meet you," I say, bowing my head. I hear scuffles around me as bowls are set down and sense the other's confusion, but one by one they lower themselves to their knees and bow their heads.

"Oh child, there's no need for that. You are the queen now. My time is over."

"Hang on a second," Lucille barks. "You're..."

"She's what? What the hell is going on?" Marcus asks.

"Balam is the original Salvator Regina. Latin for Savior Queen," I state.

Marcus's head snaps up. "She's..."

"Really old," Lucille finishes, causing Balam to let out a raspy bark.

"I like you, Lucille."

She is really old. And looks it. Would it be rude to ask how she's aged? Shouldn't she still be a fresh-faced vampire?

Lucille stands up, placing her hands on hips. Eyeing Balam suspiciously. "You know my name?"

Her indignation is hilarious.

Balam chuckles. "I know all of you." I feel a hand on my shoulder. "Please rise, my dear. We have much to discuss, including why I've aged," she says with a knowing smile. Crap, she can read my thoughts. "But first, I want you all to eat and rest. Regrettably, I can only provide you with an unlimited quantity of stars to sleep beneath this evening. Somehow, I think you'll manage, though." She grins and winks again.

There's a rustling sound coming from the back of the hut. Lucille is in front of me in seconds. Her stance signaling that she's ready to fight.

"Balam, are they here yet?" A woman, taller than Balam but with the same aged skin, shouts as she walks around the hut. "Oh, asked and answered." Her smile is as wide as Balam's.

"Itzel, come and meet Erin."

The woman, or Itzel, as I now know, takes a couple of lengthy strides over to me and takes my hand. She gives me a wink and kisses my knuckles. "Good to meet you, my Queen. We've been waiting for this day for quite a while."

Her charm and character remind me of Amelia, which makes me smile. Itzel moves to Balam and places a gentle kiss on her lips. Her hand caresses Balam's cheek. Their love is palpable. Itzel is Balam's mate, which means she was, or maybe still is, her protector, as Amelia is mine.

"I know you are desperate for answers, Erin, and I promise to provide them. But please eat the stew. You need to replenish your energy. It's full of Red."

"Organic Red. Straight from the source this morning," Itzel adds with a smile.

I *do* want answers, and I'm sure Balam can feel my impatience, but I have to trust she knows best. She's led me here when our lives are in peril. I have to believe she's going to help.

Sleeping under the stars is an experience I'd like to repeat over and over again. Looking into the universe has a unique way of putting things into perspective.

We ate the stew but were far too tired to have such an important talk, so we bid Balam and Itzel good night. Chatter was minimal as we all processed the past few days.

Surprisingly, sleep came easily and for the first time in weeks, I didn't dream.

The morning has brought dazzling rays of sun piercing through the canopy. Everyone is already awake when I finally sit up and run a hand through my hair. I should *not* have taken it out of the bun. I can feel its volume and know I look ridiculous.

"Wow," Lucille comments. She hands me a cup of fresh Red and a bowl of fruit. "That's a look."

I scowl at her because, of course, she looks perfectly put together. For once I'd like to see a Loch who is as much of a bridge troll as the rest of us when we first wake up.

"Thanks."

"You're welcome." She grins and then trots away, chuckling.

After inhaling the most delicious fruit I have ever eaten, I'm feeling a little more alive and ready to talk with Balam. As nice as it is being here, there are people waiting for us, and I want to get home. Amelia has been blocking my attempts to contact her. At first, I put it down to her needing more time to heal, but now I know there is something else going on. Chris is none the wiser. He just reiterates that she needs rest. If I can't connect with her soon, I will reach out to Victoria. Chris tells me they arrived at the bunker earlier yesterday. And if I know the Loch matriarch, she will be tending to Amelia, whether she likes it or not.

Balam and Itzel are sitting with Paula and Ricco laughing at a story Ricco is telling animatedly. Balam catches my eye and excuses herself from the conversation. "Shall we take a walk?"

"Please." My heart gives a few extra thuds as we leave the clearing and find a well-worn path.

"Do you want to ask questions, or would you like me to jump right into it?"

"Jump in, please." Yes, I have questions, but I think she will answer them all with whatever she's about to say.

"Erin, it's difficult for me to express what I need to say without feeling a profound sense of shame. Like you, I was given the ability to help vampires who fell into madness. My abilities were seen as a gift from the gods. I was celebrated and worshipped. Itzel was known as the fiercest warrior in all the land. Itzel and I embraced the adoration given to us so freely by our kind." Balam shakes her head as if she's warding off unwanted memories. "Our knowledge was limited in those days, though. The world was a brutal place and in time, Itzel and I became brutal queens. Our egos became bigger than our need to help. Our thirst for power was insatiable. We slayed anyone who opposed our word as law. We were consumed."

Wow, okay. I look at her now and struggle to marry the two sides of Balam. The scary, powerful queen and the lovely old lady. "You don't seem to be that person anymore." I'm finding it hard to picture Balam that way.

"I am not. And it was almost losing Itzel to madness that finally opened my eyes. This is important, Erin. You haven't received the gift from any God. You can use the energy that makes up life and manipulate it. I doubt you have even begun to discover your full power, and that is why I need to speak with you. It takes a strong mind and will to wield such a force. As time passes, it's easy to lose yourself to it. Itzel almost lost herself to her anger. She felt the injustice of our species' predicament intolerable. Countless humans lost their lives because of it. That guilt ate her alive until she almost did the one thing that would have destroyed me. She was on the brink of choosing to die.

"It is why we live in a place which resembles home but could never be it. Our actions had consequences to others, and ourselves. We paid a steep price, Erin. Our punishment has been to live in exile, away from everything we hold dear. Even to this day, I cannot bring myself to return home. You caught my accent? I originate from Brazil. Itzel too. We had to leave it all behind. Never to return. I do not want the same outcome for you."

My heart is no longer thudding. It's racing at a sickening speed. Amelia has voiced her anger at the way vampires are driven to madness if they can't find a mate. She has sat crying in my arms as she recounts a burning fury inside. The fear she feels at losing control. A fear I brushed aside as something that could never manifest into anything because I refused to picture Amelia becoming something so far from who she is.

Balam pulls me from my ever-darkening thoughts. "As for me. I toyed with minds, invaded dreams. No one was safe from my reach. In my head, I *was* a God."

"What made you change?"

"The night I found Itzel on the ground writhing in mental agony, begging the universe to make it stop. I dropped to my knees and prayed. I freely relinquished the power and begged Itzel's be stripped away. We weren't worthy of such a responsibility."

"And that worked?"

"Yes. There is always a choice. Which is why you need to understand the magnitude and risks you take when choosing this life. Don't get me wrong, in the right hands, your gifts are a privilege. You just need to make sure you are ready to take it on."

"Why didn't you call to me sooner?" I could have done with this information...say, two years ago.

"Because I am an old fool. I wanted nothing to do with it. I was consumed by my past failures. I was scared for Itzel. The day I felt the power rise in you, I almost collapsed. I didn't understand why I could feel it, feel you. But now I think it is my purpose to guide you. You are worthy of this gift, Erin. I have seen through your eyes the good you have done. Witnessed your tender heart. But I fear for your mate."

"Amelia? Why?"

"Itzel feels her anger. She feels her fear. There are troubling times ahead that will test you both."

My hands shake. "What do I do? I cannot lose Amelia."

"This is why I brought you here. I want to share my memories with you."

Couldn't she have just done that in the first place instead of dragging my ass across the world?

"I could walk through your mind if you agree."

Balam shakes her head. "I have to pass them on to you. Embed them in your own consciousness as if they were your own. I think that is the only way to keep you from making our mistakes over again. The only way to do that is face-to-face."

Shit, did she hear me grumbling?

"I'll feel your regret," I say quietly, bypassing my embarrassment.

"You will feel so much more than that. If you wish to be the Salvator Regina, you need to have a safeguard. A way to ground yourself when the power seems all-consuming."

"What if I don't want to be the queen?"

"Then you choose not to be."

Twenty-Three

AMELIA

We arrived at the bunker yesterday and I was promptly whisked off to the sick bay where Dr. Chord eagerly awaited me. I didn't see much point, considering the wounds had fully healed by the time we returned. However, Mother was in full...well, mother mode, so I kept my mouth shut and let Riley examine me. I also let her extract some more venom. The good doctor has been busy since Erin and I left.

"Victoria, may I have a minute with Amelia alone?"

Mother squints her eyes in disproval, but Riley doesn't flinch. "Fine. I'll be right outside."

"Better?" Riley asks me. I blow out a breath and nod.

"She's insufferable when she hovers. I'm fine. You said it yourself."

"She's just worried about her child, Amelia." Riley smiles. "I wanted a few moments alone for other reasons."

"I'm a married woman, Dr. Chord." I grin. She swats me on the arm.

"As am I." She laughs. "Glad to see your sense of humor didn't take a hit."

"No, just the rest of me." Parts Riley can't see or heal with medicine.

"Hmm. What happened out there? You're...not yourself and I don't think it's the injuries. You're almost completely healed."

I don't want to tell her. I don't want to tell anyone. I'm not ready. But how long can I avoid the questions? Mohan will be champing at the bit to delve into the details. The thought gives me palpitations.

"I'm tired, Doctor. That's all. A few good night's sleep and Erin in my arms will have me feeling like myself."

She studies my face and I know she isn't buying it, but she has the good sense to stop questioning me. "Okay, Amelia. Just know I'm here if you need to talk."

Sitting up from the examination table, I give her the best smile I can muster. "I appreciate it. Can I go now?"

"Of course. I'll check-in with you later."

Mother is waiting in the hallway as I leave the medical bay. My patience is on a tightrope, and my emotions are in crisis. I cannot stand one more second of her concerned looks and mollycoddling. It may sound harsh. I know she only wants to look after me, but being this close to her, knowing what I did, is untenable. In fact, being cooped up with all the people I love is too much. I need space to think, and I can't do that in the bunker.

I'll ask for their forgiveness later. Not just for what I did in that mine shaft, but for what I'm about to do.

Mother speaks, but I don't hear what she says as I speed past her. Everything rushes by as I head for the exit. The fresh mountain air fills my lungs, but I can't stop running. I need more distance between us. Between their expectant looks and my guilt-ridden conscience.

Erin tries to connect to me again, but I block her. We promised we wouldn't do that, but I'm breaking promises left, right, and center, so what's another one to add to the pile?

By the time I stop, tears I've refused to let go tumble down my cheeks. I don't know how to even begin moving on from this. Do I deserve to? Maybe I should just keep running. Or hide in the mountains.

Another attempt by Erin to talk to me. My resolve is crumbling. I don't deserve her worry, or her love, but I crave it. She's the only person who can give me a modicum of peace, deserved or not.

Erin, I need you.

The thought occurs before I can stop myself. My legs give out as I continue to sob. Leaning back on my knees, I look at the sky. The clear blue stretches as far as even my eyes can see.

I'm coming, Amelia.

Night has fallen, and the temperature is considerably cooler, but I stay put on my knees, looking up. Hours have passed, that much I know, and I've spent the entire time replaying that moment.

There is no easy way to tell my family what happened, but I think I'm finally ready to do it. I'm surprised Mother hasn't sent a search party out looking for me by now. Maybe Chris has already informed them of the soldier's death, and they are happy for me to be anywhere but in the bunker.

Erin deserves to find out first. Is it the coward's way to let her see what happened through my memories? At least that way I won't have to look into her eyes and see the aching disappointment she will surely feel.

"Amelia, sweetheart?" Mother's voice catches me completely off guard and I'm not ashamed to admit I scream like a little girl, falling to my ass.

"Jesus! You scared the crap out of me, Mother."

"I'm sorry, I tried to make enough noise as to avoid doing that."

"It's fine," I say, standing up. My legs are numb from staying in the same position for so long. "How did you find me?"

She gives me a coy smile. "You forget I've had quite the life. I could track you anywhere, my dear." That's a little disconcerting. "Can we talk?"

"Chris told you, didn't he?"

She nods. "Only me, and only because he could see how worried I was about you."

"Do you hate me?" I say with a crack in my voice.

She takes a step forward. "I could never hate you, Amelia. You are my child."

"But I murdered someone, Mom. I took another life in anger."

She tentatively reaches out to me. I don't pull away. "Will you tell me what happened?"

More tears fall. "I didn't see him. I didn't want to hurt anyone. I just wanted to find Mack and Jordan."

"I know, sweetie."

"He hid, but then I felt the bullet hit my back. I got so angry that I couldn't see past it. He just kept shooting, and I was on the floor. He saw my fangs. He wanted to kill me, but I killed him. I *killed* him." And then I am in my mother's embrace, my body shuddering as I release the torment that has followed me ever since it happened.

"Shh, it's okay."

I push myself away. "It's not okay!" My voice is rising, as is my anger. "I snapped a man's neck with my bare hands. It is far from okay," I roar. Blood pounds in my ears. "I knew this would happen. I felt it, in here," I say, jabbing my finger into my chest. "I knew I would become a monster."

"Amelia Loch, you are no monster."

"How can you say that?" I scream.

"Because I know your heart. That man wanted you dead. Chris told me he was like a wild animal. You defended yourself."

"Defended myself," I scoff. "Are you not listening to me?"

"I am! I'm listening to you condemn yourself. If you were a monster, Amelia, do you really think you would be racked with such guilt?"

"Maybe not. But this thing inside me, this thing that gives me the power to turn humans, also hurts people. How can I reconcile that? Is it okay to kill an asshole because I've helped a few people? Is it acceptable?"

"Amelia, he shot you multiple times. He wasn't just some guy you killed. He was a hunter, and you were his prey."

"A prey far stronger. What happens the next time I feel that rage, Mother?"

"I can't answer that. But I do know that running off and shutting us out won't help."

My hands fly to my hair in exasperation. "How the hell can I be around you all knowing—"

"I will never believe you would hurt us, Amelia. Never!"

"Then you are a fool!" I growl.

"And you are being a stubborn idiot," she replies. We stare each other down, and I'm momentarily distracted by the fact that I now know where Lucille gets her attitude from.

"I may be a stubborn idiot, but I will do what's necessary to keep you all safe, even if that means leaving."

"You would do that to us? And what of Erin? If you leave, you'll kill her. Remember what it felt like when she lost faith in us and ran away? Have you learned nothing over the years?"

Wow, Mother's kind of a bitch when she wants to be.

"Yes, you made a decision that cost a man his life, but it's not as black and white as you're making it out to be. Are you forgetting that these men were sent to find and hurt you? To hurt all vampires? God knows what they had in store for the vampires you saved after they'd finished torturing them. Do you think any of the soldiers showed Jordan and Mack any mercy? I'll answer that for you. They did not, and now those women will have to live with scars forever. Why don't you ask them if they think you're a monster? Or ask them if you saved their lives."

"I..." Have no words. My mind is a mess.

"If you *choose* to leave us. *You* are choosing to hurt us. I can't make it any clearer than that. But what the hell do I know? I'm just your mother." And then, if you believe it, she turns and storms off. I've just had my ass thoroughly handed to me.

I stand there staring at the space where my mother stood mere seconds ago. Her words repeating on a loop in my head. It's infuriating. I'm tired of thinking, tired of my brain endlessly tormenting me. Is this me, or the consequences of being the Queen's mate? I've always been a deep thinker. But I can't recall a never-ending stream of shit running through my brain before Erin bit me. Before whatever the hell is inside me reared its head.

I'm still angry. But now I'm angry at my warrior. At this whole damn thing. I never chose this. Erin never chose this. And yet, here we are. Stuck with a power that is as dangerous and destructive as it is helpful.

It took me so long to get to a place where I believed I had embraced this part of myself. But I should have listened to my fears because all it has brought us is trouble.

That's not true, my love.

It is true.

Be patient, Amelia. I have so much to tell you.

Does this mean she knows what I did?

I've still not found the nerve to return to the bunker.

Instead, I've paced, seethed, cried, and laughed at the complete mess that seems to be me. I have so many thoughts racing around, I can't make head nor tale of how I really feel anymore.

The sun set and then rose again. I feel Erin getting closer. I feel her warmth washing over me as she tries to calm my frayed nerves. We should never have split up. Or at least we should have kept in contact. Maybe then I wouldn't have done what I did. Erin would have broken through to me. She's the only one who could.

Is this what it's like to go slowly mad?

"You're not going mad, baby."

My eyes close as her voice wraps around me. I daren't turn around in case she's not really there. I'm scared my desperation is playing tricks on my mind.

"Turn around, Amelia. I'm here."

I turn slowly, praying Erin is really standing there waiting to catch me. Her hair is up in its standard high ponytail. She looks tired, but her eyes sparkle with joy as she regards me. I'm sure I look like crap after spending a day and night out here.

"You're here?"

"I am, honey." She opens her arms, and I fall into her. "We have so much to talk about. But for now, I just want to hold you."

I want her to hold me and never let me go. It's the only way I won't shatter into a million pieces.

Twenty-Four

ERIN

Wow, I have so much to unpack, so much to process. The transfer of memories was far beyond anything I was expecting. I'm used to experiencing other people's dreams, even their memories, but not like that. But I didn't have time to process what had happened because the second I heard Amelia's broken voice in my head, I had to go. Nothing and no one was going to stop me.

Lucille didn't put up a fight, not after Balam told us to go, and quickly. Itzel said she felt Amelia's turmoil, and my heart sank. Knowing what I knew, my first instinct was to panic. I'd seen and felt Itzel longing to die. Knowing that's something that could befall Amelia almost overwhelmed me.

We ran through the jungle as fast as our legs could take us. I arrived at the airport before the rest of the group, which gave me a little time to take a few deep breaths. My mind was a mess. Balam told me there would be trying times ahead for Amelia and me. To be honest, those times were starting a little earlier than expected.

Gone were the toy planes. Lucille organized a private jet to fly us home. God knows how she managed it while bolting through the jungle. We didn't make any stops. I couldn't have cared less if the Special Forces or God herself found out where I was. I'd have fought them all to get back to Amelia.

Tired and on edge, I counted the hours as we drew closer to the US. My leg wouldn't stop bouncing, and my heart gave a jolt now and then when I felt slivers of Amelia's heartache. What the hell happened? God, we were so stupid to keep each other at arm's length. I know we thought it was the right thing for both of us. No distractions, but in hindsight, it was foolish.

The second the plane landed, we were out and whisked away. Lucille had really done a fantastic job getting everything sorted at such short notice. Maybe she could see the anxiety on my face, or the way I winced every time I felt Amelia.

We were taken to a rendezvous point where Jeremy waited to escort us back to the bunker. It was a silent ride, with everyone feeling on edge. I hadn't told them about Amelia's state of mind, but it didn't take a genius to figure out something was very wrong.

I hugged them all when we arrived at the cabin. They watched me with quizzical eyes as I turned away from the safety of the bunker and headed into the mountains. Amelia's soul guiding me every step of the way until I finally found her.

My heart wanted to break. Her body looked racked with fatigue and pain. I knew it wasn't from the gunshot wounds. But the real heartache happened when she turned toward me. Her eyes, the eyes I am so used to seeing with love shining through, were dull and haunted. She looked at me as if I were an apparition. It took every ounce of strength not to break down in front of her. I had to be the strong one. Amelia was falling apart, and I had to be there to catch her.

It's only now, as my arms wrap around her, she's able to believe her own eyes. She sobs into my neck, her body racked with pain. Tears come to my eyes as I hold her tightly. I feel like such a fool for blocking her out. Whatever happened has devastated her, and she's gone through it alone.

Time passes but I pay it no mind. I'll stand here forever if that's what she needs. I guide us to the ground when I feel her legs quiver. She's so tired. I can't believe she's still conscious. I stroke her hair and inhale her scent. It's as much for me as it is a comfort for her. I can't explain how much I have missed her. I'll never be apart from her like that again. No matter what the situation or consequences, I choose to be by Amelia's side. Damn my responsibilities as this so-called savior queen.

She pulls away from me, her eyes bloodshot and swollen. "I'm so happy you're here. But I'm not sure you will be as happy to be with me after I tell you what I've done."

Ignoring the fact my heart is beating double time, I gently stroke her face with my fingertips. "There is nothing you can tell me that will make me change the way I see you, Amelia."

"You don't know that," she says, her voice cracking. "I'm a monster."

There is only one reason she would call herself that. "No. You are not. You are good, and kind, and loving."

"I... Erin, I killed someone." She's looking at me like I'm about to jump away from her, horrified.

I keep stroking her cheek tenderly. "Tell me what happened, my love."

She furrows her eyebrows as she tries to work out why I'm not reacting. Eventually, she drops her gaze to the ground. I know she's feeling shame. She rubs her palms up and down her thighs in agitation.

"Tell me," I plead.

I listen as she opens up. She tells me every step of her journey, searching for our friends. She cries as she recounts the way things happened in the mine. She berates herself and tells me what she should have done differently. I let her rage and sob some more until she's slumped in my arms once more.

"I need you to trust me, Amelia, when I tell you that what you are feeling is more than what you think."

"What does that mean?"

It means I have so, so much to tell her. To share with her, I don't know where to start.

"It means we need to get back to the bunker, and you need to rest because I've learned things about us that will help you understand all these conflicting feelings."

"They'll all want to know what happened, and I can't, Erin. I thought I was ready, but I can't tell them. I can't keep reliving it. It's enough that I'm unable to escape the memories. It hurts so much more to say it out loud."

I'm reminded of the vast difference in our height when I attempt to help her up. "No one will ask you anything, I promise. Please trust me."

"I trust you with my life, you know that," she replies. Her voice is only a whisper. I suspect she's close to losing it after so much crying and raving.

We slowly make our way back to the cabin. Amelia wrings her hands as we approach the door. I take them in mine and kiss each knuckle. "Come. You need rest."

I reached out to Victoria the moment we started our trek down the mountain. I made it very clear that no one was to approach Amelia or me. I know Victoria will make damn sure that we are left alone. A small smile graces my lips when I think of her going all Momma Loch on a bunker full of vampires.

There's no one to greet us as we enter the common room and make our way toward our bedroom. Amelia is jumpy and almost sprints the last few meters. Once we are safely locked away, she slumps on the bed.

Lifting her face, I place a gentle kiss on her lips. "Let's take a shower, baby."

Without protest, she allows me to lead her to the bathroom. I strip her first, taking in every inch of her body. There are no signs of the gunshot wounds, but I still trace my fingers over her abdomen. I can feel where the bullets hit her. Not physically. I can feel the pain when I trace over certain spots. Amelia keeps her eyes closed, and I know she's reliving it again.

Turning on the shower, I gently guide her into the warm spray. Slipping out of my clothes, I waste no time wrapping my arms around her from the back. My head rests between her shoulders. For a while, we stand there and let the heated water soothe our muscles. Then I feel her sob again.

The water turns cool before we leave and get dry. Forgoing clothes, we climb into bed and hold each other. I know I should share what I learned from Balam, but I really don't think her mind can take it right now. *I almost couldn't cope with the emotions I felt through the transfer.*

The silence is making her uncomfortable. She fidgets and sniffs a few times. Lucille's karaoke rendition springs to mind for some reason, so I hum it.

Amelia shifts her head and stares at me. "I had that song going 'round my head the other day."

I smile. "Ah yes. It was Lucille's choice of song on the karaoke machine."

Her eyebrows reach for the sky. "Lucille sang? On a karaoke machine?"

"Oh yes. Several times."

"My sister Lucille? The one with a permanent stick up her bitchy ass?"

I chuckle and nod. "Marcus, too. I wondered if the Lochs had a secret karaoke fetish or something."

"Um, absolutely not. Lucille? Really?"

I smile. "There's a lot more than meets the eye with that one."

"What does that mean?"

"Oh no. I can't say anymore through fear of disembowelment."

She shakes her head, but for the first time since seeing her again, she cracks a small smile. Her head rests back on my shoulder. "Did you get what we need? To stop the president."

"Yes, but all in good time, love. Sleep now. We're both going to need our strength."

It's not the reunion I'd envisioned. But I'm just grateful we made it back to one another. Amelia slips into slumber, but I don't follow. She's going to need me for a while. I can already feel the nightmare brewing. I don't need to enter her mind to know that. So I lay there stroking her back and kissing her hair. As predicted, she whimpers and jerks. I close my eyes and let my soul cast out a comforting wave of calm and love. Her body settles and her mind relaxes. It's several hours later that I finally give up the fight and fall asleep.

I'm startled awake by Amelia screaming. She's sweat-soaked and clutching the bed sheet. I promised I wouldn't enter her dreams again without consent, but I can't lay here watching this. Placing my forehead against her, I slip into her mind. I'm in a dark room. Amelia is on the floor bleeding. A man is on top of her. A gun in one of his hands. There is so much blood. Amelia screams, her fangs bared, and her eyes blood red. The man tries to put the barrel of the gun to her head, but Amelia reaches for his neck. It's over in seconds. I hear the snap and see him slump forward. And then I see Amelia's eyes return to their normal color and the realization of what she's just done hit her.

I can't watch anymore, and I can't let Amelia keep torturing herself like this. Conjuring my favorite memory, I push out Amelia's nightmare and replace it with the sun-soaked beach and ocean that I love so much. It's the place Amelia took me on her bike. We've done so much together and seen so many things, but this moment is one I will always treasure. I walk to Amelia, who looks confused. She sits up, scanning her body, looking for her wounds, but they aren't there. She's in a bikini, her hair gently blowing in the wind with sunglasses on. It's not a permanent solution to her pain, but just for tonight, I want her to find some solace. I lower myself between her legs and sit back until I feel her chest. She's a little slow to relax, but eventually her long arms snake around me and she rests her head on my shoulder.

We sit there staring out at the horizon. It's not permanent, but for now it's enough. Tomorrow will arrive before we know it, and then the hard work begins.

Twenty-Five

AMELIA

The lamp is on low when I open my eyes, casting a gentle glow around the room. My eyelids feel puffy and I'm sure I look dreadful, but I don't care. I only care that Erin is still beside me, softly snoring. She took away my nightmare last night, and I'm so very grateful. It's amazing what a few hours of truly restful sleep can do. I'm still filled with heat from the sunshine we lay beneath as we watched the tide sweep in.

The events of the last few days are lingering on the edge of my mind, and that's where they can stay for a while. I know it's not the last time I'll feel shitty. The guilt will stay with me forever, but it feels a little more manageable with

Erin here. I wonder if she's the one doing the protecting now. To feel so calm after nearly breaking down yesterday suggests she is taking some of the negative emotion from me. Do I deserve it? I'm not so sure, but I know the weight of my shame was close to breaking me.

She stirs, her gorgeous eyes blink rapidly as they adjust to the light. My god, she's magnificent. I lower my lips to hers and nuzzle her nose. Her hand comes to my face, and she caresses my cheek, just as she did yesterday. We spend a few moments soaking each other in before our mouths meet in a slow kiss.

Usually our kisses lead to more, but as calm as I feel, I'm not in the right headspace to make love to her. Erin reads me and pulls back. "There will be time for that, my love. When you feel ready."

It scares me to think I'll never be ready. Everything inside feels distorted and wrong.

"I'm sorry," I say, breathing into her mouth as I reclaim her lips. We stay locked together for a few minutes. We were apart for mere days, but it might as well have been years.

"You don't need to apologize, baby. We've both had a rough few days."

I nuzzle her nose one more time. "Are you ready to tell me?" She searches my face. I know she's weighing up if I can handle whatever it is she has to share. "You can show me if it's easier?"

"No. I mean, there are things I need to share with you. But we need to talk first."

"Okay."

She gives me one last kiss before pushing up the bed until she's resting against the headboard. "I'm going to get us some breakfast. When I'm back, we'll get to it, okay?"

My body needs sustenance, and a few minutes alone to prepare for what Erin has to tell me. It's obviously big. I dress in sweatpants and a t-shirt while Erin is gone. Comfort is key.

She returns with several bottles of Red and a stack of pancakes. We drink and eat silently until we've both had our fill. I'm patiently waiting for Erin to begin.

"We found the hut and the person living there," she says. I nod, encouraging her to continue. "Amelia, I met the original Salvator Regina and her mate."

I'm glad we've finished eating, otherwise I think I would have just choked. "I'm sorry, what now?"

"Yup. Both are still alive and looking well for their ages."

I wasn't expecting that. "Okay. And what did they have to say?"

I'm asking, as if she had a quick chat with someone at the grocery store.

"This is where it gets intense." She wiggles her butt to get comfy. She's so cute. "So, Balam, that's the Queen, called me to her for two reasons. One to give me the key to stopping the madness we're in right now."

"And the second?" I don't think I'm going to like this bit.

Erin clears her throat. "To warn me. Us."

I wipe my hands down my face. "Against what?"

If she tells me we're going to have to fight a war or something as equally awful, I'm going to scream. Have we not gone through enough?

"Against ourselves, my love."

Oh, god I was right. "Explain, please."

"Stay with me, Amelia. I can't share this with you if you're not one hundred percent present. I know you feel like spiraling, but it won't help us. Not right now."

"Okay, I'm good. I'm fine. What's the warning?"

She eyes me for a second longer before speaking. "Balam and Itzel, her mate, didn't exactly treat their gifts with respect."

"Meaning."

"Okay. We can manipulate energy."

"Uh Huh."

"We're not inhabited by some ancient magic or anything. I'm able to Night Walk, and you can protect. Plus, other stuff I know we haven't discovered yet."

So far, I understand. "What about our venom? And the fact we can turn the Fallen and human mates?"

"We can extract healing properties in our bodies and turn them into something physical. We have something that is missing in the Fallen and their mates, which allows them to bond and become immortal."

"Right. So are we products of evolution or something more?"

I don't know why I need to know, really. The fact is, we have these gifts and frankly, I'm pissed off about it.

"Well, we're all made up of molecules and energy, so I still think it's evolution. We're variants, remember. One-of-a-kind pair, as Riley put it."

How is she so calm? This is batshit crazy.

"Riiight. Continue."

She raises her eyebrow at me. "I know it sounds bonkers, but is it any more bonkers than thinking we were the reincarnated versions of two ancient queens?"

"This Balam and Itzel, *were* regarded as queens. They had legends written about them. I'm guessing we'll have to endure the same."

She huffs, and I roll my lips to stop a smile forming. I love it when she gets all sassy. "Yes, but we're not actual reincarnated queens. We've just got the same variants in our genome as Balam and Itzel, I'm guessing. I mean, sure, Balam referred to me as Salvator Regina, but I think that's out of habit. But I know we have a choice in the matter. We still have free will. So maybe it's not all to do with evolution."

She's rambling, and it's adorable. I chuckle as she continues to think out loud, more to herself than me. She bites her lip in concentration before shaking herself out of her reverie.

"The fact is, we can manipulate energy, but it's a heavy burden to bear. It is overwhelming. I think you'll agree."

Damn right, I agree! "It is. But how does this help me deal with what I've done?"

"This is where I need to share Balam and Itzel's memories with you. But listen, honey. It's not a simple stroll through their lives. They will become a part of you. You'll feel as if their lives were once yours. That includes their emotions."

"Will this help me understand?" God, I hope so.

"Yes."

"Then do it." I've no idea what's about to happen, but I trust Erin when she says this is necessary.

"Close your eyes. Find your light and wait for me. This is going to be hard."

My skin prickles with anticipation. I center myself and wait. I'm pretty good at finding my light now. It's all the meditation. Although, when I reach for it this time, I regard it differently. It no longer feels safe. I know what that energy can manifest into. I feel Erin's presence. She hovers close by, a little hesitant to close the distance.

It's going to feel like a download of images and emotions. It'll be fast and painful. Whatever you do, try to stay calm. I'm right here.

Bracing myself, I open myself to her. It starts before I'm really prepared. Thousands of images pouring into me. It's disorientating and I'm feeling untethered. Then a wave of emotion slams into me and I cry out. My god, so much anger, it's excruciating. I feel everything. It's too much. I want it to stop, but I can already feel the memories embedding themselves into my very fiber. They latch on and I'm helpless to stop it.

One memory sears itself into my brain. Itzel, killing a group of men in a blind fury. I feel every second. The blood coating her face drips down my own. She howls in fury as she tears through them one by one.

No more!

I scream it at the top of my lungs but there is no respite. Wave after wave of memories continue to flood me, accompanied by their hellish emotions. Just when I think I'm going to collapse, everything falls silent. Everything is dark.

The room spins as I open my eyes. I'm going to vomit. Staggering to my feet, I blindly stumble toward where I hope the bathroom is. Erin's arm wraps around me and she helps me to the toilet. I empty my stomach and continue to wretch.

"Just breathe, baby. Just breathe."

I don't know how long it takes before I'm confident I can move, but eventually Erin helps me back to our room and onto the bed. I'm slick with sweat and my head is pounding.

How on earth did she think I'd feel better after that? If anything, it has reaffirmed my fear that I will lose control again. Itzel was an unhinged animal. Far beyond what I did.

However, I felt her anger. It is the same anger I feel. The same red haze I felt when I squeezed the soldier's throat.

"Amelia, I can see you spiraling. Remember what I said. I need you to remain calm and rational. I need to explain what it means to us."

"It means I'm a fucking maniac, Erin. You saw what I'm going to become!"

"No, I didn't, and neither did you. Please calm down and let me explain."

Her eyes are pleading with me. She puts her hand on my heart. Those blue eyes bore into me, waiting for me to comply.

After several large inhales, I gather myself. "I'm calm." Sort of.

"Yes, the memories you saw were of Itzel losing herself but," she forges on when I open my mouth to interject. "If you wade through all her other memories, all the carnage, you will notice the difference in your experience. She felt no remorse or fear of what she was becoming. It was only when her fractured soul couldn't take the pain of her guilt any longer did she change."

I shake my head. "But you said she didn't feel remorse. How could she feel guilty?"

"Because as much as she didn't care at the time, there was still a part of her that remained conscious of all the pain she was causing. Not just to others, but to herself. She'd strayed so far away from who she was. You saw how power hungry they both became. It consumed everything they were until they were unrecognizable."

"I still don't understand."

"The part of you that is the Amelia I know and love far outweighs the anger, honey. You've only ever hurt someone in self-defense. And I know that doesn't make it any easier to digest what's happened lately, but if you sit with it, you'll see you are not a monster."

"But these memories are a warning?"

"They are. And not just for you, babe. You saw the disregard Balam had for anyone, human and vampire. She did as she pleased. Manipulated minds, even fracturing people's reality until they were nothing but an incoherent mess. Look how easily I slipped into your dream and took over. I have to be aware too, love. What we have is powerful and dangerous. But if we continue to use it for what it was always intended for. Helping the Fallen and their mates, we will still be Erin and Amelia. Or..."

"Or? There's another option."

She nods. "Or we can give it up. Relinquish our roles as 'The Savior Queens' and go back to being regular old vamps."

I'm sorry, what? "Is that why Balam and Itzel aren't…"

"Yes. But they didn't sit down and have a rational discussion. Balam begged for their abilities to be taken away. She couldn't watch Itzel kill herself."

"Jesus." We have a chance to go back. I can't believe it. "But if it's evolution—"

"Babe. I don't know how it all works. All I know is we have the choice. Just like we do regarding our immortality."

"What do you want Erin?" This isn't just about me, and I'd do well to remember that a little more often.

"I want to tackle the president first before we talk about it. But we will talk. This is a big decision."

"Okay. So we're going to sideline this for a while."

Erin crawls into my lap and wraps her hands around my shoulders. "Only until the next job is done."

"So how do we use what Balam gave us to stop the president from exterminating us?"

She smiles at me and pecks my nose with her lips. "Simple. We use knowledge as a weapon."

Right. Simple.

Twenty-Six

ERIN

"Simple. We use knowledge as a weapon."

I say it like it's the easiest thing in the world. Well, I guess it is really. If the president doesn't step down after I execute my plan, I don't know if anything will get her there.

The discussion with Amelia feels like the tip of the iceberg as far as things we still have to learn and discuss. We have massive decisions to make that will no doubt change our lives, but to do that, I think we need to spend some time with Balam and Itzel. That can't happen until we get this crap resolved.

"That simple?" Amelia pulls me closer. Her hand instinctively makes small circles on my lower back.

"Well, the idea is simple. The follow through might need a bit of thought." Like how the hell we're going to get within one hundred feet of the president? "We need to see her in person."

"Easy, I'm sure we're on the White House guest list by now," Amelia deadpans. I swat her shoulder.

"Obviously not. Hence why we need a plan."

I'm happy to see a genuine smile on Amelia's face, even when she's being kind of an ass. I'll be honest, I was worried for a while. She seemed so lost in her grief, which is why I had to share Balam's memories with her.

They may only be the CliffsNotes of what we need to know, but I couldn't think of another way to pull her out of her dark hole. It scared me to see her like that. Amelia isn't seeking power. She doesn't want that, which is why I know she will be okay. I hope she'll take what she's seen and come to the same conclusion. Yes, we need to remain cautious, and we have a lot to discuss, but right here and now, Amelia is still the loving soul I met years ago.

"Reaching out to our contact seems the best option. He can tell us when it will be the best time."

"That's our first call, then. As soon as we have a window, we take it. This needs to be done, so we can move on," I say, laying my head on her chest. Our souls hum with a quiet satisfaction as we simply hold each other. Sometimes it's the simple things that mean the most.

"Do you want to tell me the entire plan? I mean, I get the gist that you're going to share something with her, but what?"

I sigh. "Everything. I'm going to show her everything."

She shifts, lifting my head up. "Um, that doesn't really make it any clearer, my love."

I lean forward and kiss her. "Can we just be here, together, loving each other for a little while longer? I don't want to talk about her, or Balam, or anyone else for that matter. I just need it to be us."

We stay wrapped up together for another two hours. The bunker is probably a hive of activity, and no doubt there are more than a few people who would like to hear from us, but the one thing I've learned over the past few days is that I can't and won't put anyone before Amelia and me.

"I think I need to talk to them," Amelia whispers into the silence. "We can't keep hiding away. I can't keep running away."

"You're not running, baby. You're processing a really shitty thing that's happened. Take all the time you need. You don't owe anyone an explanation."

I feel her hiccup and a small sob escape. "Not even his family? That's what gets me the most, Erin. What if I've created a widow? Left a child without their father?"

What can I say? Those are possibilities. "Do you want to find out? Instead of guessing."

"Yes. I need to know what damage I've caused."

God, my heart is hurting so much. Her devastation is palpable. "Amelia..."

"Say it. Please."

Should I say this? Will she see it for what it is, an act of love, or will she get defensive? "I...I can take this away, if you want."

She shuffles me off her lap. Her face is a picture of confusion. "What do you mean?"

Clearing my throat, I take her hands. "I can take the pain, guilt, and shame away. All of it, if you want."

She stares at me for long enough that I start to feel antsy. "You mean alter my memory or something?"

"Sort of. I can make the memory fade so it doesn't feel so raw, or I can make it vanish altogether." Although I got little time with Balam, there was enough for her to share a few things I'd yet to discover about my abilities. Standing, she paces. For once I can't read her. She looks agitated, but is that toward me? "Amelia, I'm sorry."

"No," she says, turning to face me. "Thank you. I appreciate your offer, but I can't let myself off that easy."

"And I can't watch you drown in guilt," I shoot back.

She nods and takes my hand. "I know. And I get I need to work this out. I will, I promise. But I can't work through it by having you take my memories or feelings. If I want to still be me, still the Amelia I remember before all this, I have to work through it my way."

"Okay. I won't mention it again."

"I love you for offering. Now I need to stop wallowing and start facing this head-on. Shall we see my parents?"

We share another embrace before Amelia takes my hand, and we head into the common room. She already looks stronger, and I know she means what she says when she tells me she'll work through it.

Amelia is scooped up as soon as her family claps eyes on her. I stand back and let them give her what I know she needs. Victoria is the last to get her arms around her daughter, and for a moment, I think we're going to have to pry them apart with a crowbar.

Chris is also with us. He steps forward and whispers something in Amelia's ear. And if I'm not mistaken, I think her shoulders drop a fraction. But not in a bad way. It's like some of the tension has been relieved. I'll ask her about it when we get a second alone. If she wanted me to hear it, she'd have let me in.

Mohan bustles into the room. He makes a beeline for Amelia. "Are you okay?"

Amelia smiles, which is good. I know she hasn't totally forgiven him for all this. "I will be. But we need to talk."

"Chris has given his account of the events, Amelia. You had no choice."

She tenses. "There is always a choice. But I don't want to talk about that right now. Erin and I need to update the council."

Mohan nods. "Let's gather everyone, then."

We all gather in the common room. It sucks to be back here. The gray concrete is depressing. The faster we figure a way to get to the president, the faster Amelia and I can get out of here.

"Thank you for joining us," Amelia begins. I'm so proud of her. She's not shying away, even though she knows people have heard about that event in the mine. She's standing with her head held high, commanding the room. "Erin's trip seems to have given us what we need to end this. Now we need to get to the woman herself. We need a private audience with the president."

There's a smattering of chit chat.

"I'll call our man on the inside," Mohan says. "Once we have some sort of schedule, it will make it easier to plan."

Lucille steps forward. "Sorry to be blunt, but why are you here discussing it with this lot?" She gestures to an almost outraged group of councilmen and women. "No offense, but none of them can do a damn thing to help. You two can slip into the White House with no input from any of us. So do it. Stop fucking around and finish this."

"Luce, we have a hierarchy for a reason," Amelia states, her back molars grinding together.

"Oh, fuck the hierarchy. If you really believed that you wouldn't get pissy every time someone bows to you. This is a unique situation where we don't need to be stopping every fart's end to have a goddam discussion. You two have the key to bringing peace back to our community. Get out of this godforsaken bunker and do it!"

Amelia takes a step toward her sister, but I get a hold of her forearm before they can start going at it. So much for Lucille dropping her bitch barriers.

"Lucille's right!" Victoria almost looks as shocked as the rest of us with her outburst. But in true Victoria Loch fashion, she recovers quickly and looks the epitome of cool and collected. "You know I have great respect for our customs and laws. We have a council for a reason. But my rambunctious daughter has a point. Only Amelia and Erin can stop this. They don't need our permission to move forward. This is their arena, not ours. All this updating and debating is just wasting time."

"Thanks, Mom." Lucille grins. "So, as I was saying. As soon as you know where she'll be, just do your thing. You've got more power in your pinkies than any of us could ever imagine having." She glares at Amelia, daring her to respond.

Simon steps forward next. What is going on?

"May I say something?"

"Of course," I respond. I'm eager to hear his thoughts and intrigued to see where the conversation is going.

"I am a council member. In the community, I am seen as a pillar of strength. As a vampire, as someone to be respected. Before coming to this bunker, I didn't deserve any of it, and if I may be so bold, I think there are several members who are in the same boat." More rumblings from the crowd. "We need a council, but I believe an overhaul is required."

Okay, so we're completely off track now. I guess we're about to shake up the vampire leadership then.

"Why?" Mohan asks, but he isn't angry. He's intrigued.

"Because we've become complacent. I'm a council member because of the influence of my father. Many of us are here because of either money or power. How is that any different from the humans?" More chatter. "The council was formed to make decisions regarding the safety and well-being of our kind. I'm sure other councils around the globe have fallen into the same trap we have. How can we be effective leaders when we are so disconnected from our people? Case in point. The uprising to declare ourselves to the humans. It didn't come from a longing to be out in the world. It came from a place of arrogance. Let's not pretend we wanted anything more than to peacock how brilliant we are to the humans. We have the same rights as them. We work hard. We have loving families. The only difference is what we call ourselves."

"But we're hiding," Mohan states. "That's why we told the president."

"Hiding? I'm not so sure, Grand Master. We're living. We're thriving, and with the help of Erin and Amelia, we are bringing our Fallen brethren back into the community. What more is there? We source our own food with no concern. There is no reason to cause an uproar in the world. In our world. Unless it's to prove something to the humans."

Mohan looks contemplative for several minutes. It's the longest silence I've ever encountered. "I move to call an election," he begins. "When Erin and Amelia have completed their task, we will call for a dissolution of the council, and my own position. Mr. Becker is right. We need leadership that is one hundred percent focused on the welfare of our kind. Whether they be CEOs or bakers.

Nepotism has no place here. And I'd like to apologize for not doing anything about it sooner."

With the room in stunned silence, Mohan turns to Amelia and me. "If you need anything, reach out. Good luck." And then he leaves.

Amelia turns to me with wide eyes. *What the hell was all that?* Her voice is near screeching point in my head.

I don't know what that was, or where it came from. I haven't got the patience to deal with politics. We've got a president to catch.

Twenty-Seven

AMELIA

I'm not sure what the hell just happened? One minute we're updating the council and the next the entire political system is being overhauled. I know I told Simon to do better, but Jesus, I wasn't expecting that.

As for Lucille and my mother, I'm still in shock. Not so much about Lucille. Her outbursts should be expected, especially if they're designed to irritate me. But my mother! I never thought I'd see the day she would go against our customs.

Erin all but pushes me back to our bedroom. I'll be so glad when we can leave this place. Perhaps it will happen sooner than expected. In fact, I'm going to make sure that happens. I'm so done with running.

"Well, that took an interesting turn," she quips, throwing herself on the bed.

"Didn't it just. The timing could have been better though." I chuckle. It's not funny, really. We've already got so much happening in our world. Maybe right now isn't the time to be thinking about elections and the council.

"It's not for us to worry about, baby."

I stand with my hands on my hips. "Of course it is. We're a part of this community."

She rolls her eyes at me. "Yes. But as you heard, there aren't going to be any changes until we finish with the president. So, right now, it *isn't* for us to worry about."

I suppose she's right. "Fair. So how do we feel about having free rein on this?"

"Lucille and your mother have a point. The time for talking is done. We are the only ones who have the abilities and strength to end this. We need to stop talking about it and get it done."

Erin is delicious when she gets like this. Her assertiveness is so sexy. I wait for the familiar feeling of guilt to wash over me. It's no secret the past few days have left me feeling as if I don't deserve to feel anything but shame. I still have that guilt, but Chris somewhat helped me let go a little. He informed me that the soldier I killed had no family. In fact, he was on a final warning for his conduct. He was career military. Two divorces, both with battery allegations made against him. No children, thank god. This does *not* negate what I have done. He was still a person. Just not a very nice one.

"You're thinking hard over there, honey." Erin props herself up on her elbows and looks at me curiously. I know she can see the difference in me from when we left here this morning to now. There's no need to keep it from her, so I let the information filter through to her mind. She closes her eyes and sighs.

"I'm very pleased. But I know you will still need time to get over it."

"I will. But it helped. He was a dirtbag. However, I still should have controlled myself. I know that."

I'm still not entirely sure how Itzel's memories are supposed to help me understand. I guess Erin wanted me to see how different I am from her, and the choices she made. My distress at what I have done is the opposite of Itzel's elation. She reveled in the destruction until her consciousness finally broke with the weight of blood she'd shed.

Okay, so maybe I *do* understand, and maybe it has helped me see a different side. God knows I could only envision my worst nightmare coming true. Now, I'm cautiously optimistic, I won't become Itzel. Even more so now, I know we have a choice. We could give it all up. Is that what I want?

"We're putting that to one side, remember?" Erin gently scolds. She's right. There will be a time to dive back into all that. Now isn't it.

Nodding my head, I begin to undress. I will put everything to one side. Now I'm going to do what I should've done the second Erin was back in my arms. I'm going to reclaim her. I've been a mess, and I know I haven't been the mate she's deserved for a long time now. My moods are unpredictable, and yet through it all, this woman has never flinched from giving me everything I need.

It's my turn to give her what she needs. I know she's suppressing her wants. She's done that for a while now, too. I'm not the only one who went through a stressful and scary few days. I'm not the only one of us that felt our distance keenly. Erin missed me as much as I did her. Yet she's kept her distance to help me. Again.

I may feel broken, but for Erin, I'll patch myself together, even if it's temporary. However, I'm not being completely altruistic. Selfishly, I know her touch and essence on my skin will help me heal.

"Um, Amelia, what are you doing?"

I snap open my pants and push them to my ankles before stepping out of them. My t-shirt is already on the ground, along with my bra. Curling my thumbs under the waistband of my panties, I glide them over my legs slowly. Erin's pupils dilate and she licks her lips.

Instead of answering, I part my legs and snake my hand into my folds. I don't want to talk or analyze my feelings anymore. I want to concentrate on us. On the look of pure desire in my mate's eyes. My fingers skim over my clit, which twitches. Amazing how quickly my body responds when I let my heart take over from my head.

"Mmmm, I'm so wet for you." My eyes flutter as I explore myself further. The bedsheets rustle as Erin perches on her knees.

"Keep going, baby."

Forcing my eyes back open, I watch in wonder as Erin plays with herself. Her eyes never leaving my pussy. It's embarrassing how fast I'm tumbling toward a climax. But I'm not ready for this to be over. Stilling my fingers, I stride over to her, stopping the protest from leaving her mouth with my tongue.

I make quick work of her clothes. Our breaths are ragged as I dance my hands over her skin. This needs to be about Erin's pleasure. After pinching her nipples, I gently push her down until her back hits the mattress. Taking her knees in my hands, I pull her until her pussy is almost off the edge of the bed. Dropping to the ground, I place both legs over my shoulders.

She glistens in the lamplight. I love it when she whimpers in need. She uses one hand to massage her breasts and the other to grip the sheets in anticipation of the pleasure she knows is coming. My tongue glides up the inside of her thigh. Using my thumbs, I hold her open. Her scent washes over me and I breathe deeply. I blow a little air over her sensitive clit, grinning when she jerks and curses.

The first swipe of my tongue has me moaning. Nectar drips from her, and I plan to clean up every drop. Her hips move as I take another taste. I know she wants me to take her hard and fast, but teasing her, making her wait is so much more satisfying, and her orgasm will be so much more powerful for a little edging.

When her hand fists my hair, I know she's getting frustrated. I've brought her to the brink now several times, but backed off before she could tip over.

"Please, baby," she pants.

"Please, what?"

"Please let me come. I can't take any more teasing."

"Can you take my fingers?"

"Yes. Four, I need four."

Coating my fingers, I gently push them in until I'm three knuckles deep inside of her. Her groan sends electricity straight to my own needy center. It would be so easy to drop my hand and touch myself, but I don't. She adjusts to me with ease. Stroking her G-spot, I begin to move in and out. My position isn't great, so I stand, bending her legs toward her chest. The shift causes her breath to hitch as I pick up my pace. I'm almost curled over her body now, and my pussy is rubbing against the back of my hand. Biting my lip, I'm sure I've pierced the skin as I try to hold off my own excitement, but it's hard when the friction is so fucking delectable.

"A-amelia...oh, oh yes!"

I put my mouth to better use by sucking in her left nipple. We're both making incoherent sounds as I push a little harder and faster. Her body clamps and vibrates, flooding my hand. As soon as her back arches, I know it's over. Her scream echoes through the room. She rides out her orgasm with my hand still buried inside, motionless. My head rests on her chest as I catch my breath.

"I...I wasn't expecting that," she says.

"I wanted to make you feel good, my love."

"Oh, you succeeded. But I thought you'd need more time."

Lifting my head, I slowly extricate myself from her and position my hands on either side of her head. "I needed to get out of my head and stop being selfish."

"You're—"

"We've both been through it recently, Erin. I missed you so damn much. This should have been the first thing we did as soon as we were back together."

"Amelia..."

"I know, I know. But it's time to move on. I'm ready to get our lives back."

"Me too. But I need to touch you first."

"Have me however you want, my love. And then we're getting out of this place."

Erin is still sleeping, so I shower and head out to look for Mohan. I meant what I said. We're leaving here as soon as possible. Our friends and family are safe, so it's time to stop running. Hopefully Mohan's contact has the president's schedule for us.

"Amelia, just the vampire queen I was looking for." I wince at the name.

"No more of that, Mohan," I say with authority. He looks at me, a little confused. "There's much to explain, but that's for another time. However, I need you to stop referring to us as queens."

I'm sure Balam and Itzel adored their titles, but it's time to retire them for good. We are no queens.

"But—"

"No buts. We are not reincarnated queens. We are vampires with the ability to help. No more, no less. Please spread the word. No more bowing, no more worshipping. It all stops."

He doesn't need to know any more than that.

He looks taken aback but doesn't push further. "Here is the information you need."

I take the sheet of paper and give it a once over. The president isn't scheduled to leave the White House for the next few days, and I see the First Lady has a conference out of state in two days' time. That's it. That's our window. We need her alone. The last thing I want to do is scare her wife half to death.

"Thank you, Mohan. This is helpful. Erin and I will be leaving in the next few hours. I'd appreciate it if you kept that quiet. We don't need the fanfare."

His eyebrows pinch together. "Right. If that's what you want. Will you tell your family?"

"Of course." I shake his hand. "Take care of everyone."

He goes to bow, but my raised eyebrows stop him in his tracks. "Good luck."

"That looked tense," Marcus says from behind me as we watch Mohan leave.

"Not really. Is the family awake?"

"Of course."

We take off toward the dining room my family seems to have claimed as their own. My heart swells when I see them all. It will be difficult to leave them again, but this time I know it won't be for long.

"Good morning everyone."

Mother stands and hugs me. Her worry for me is palpable. Father gives me a wink and a smile.

"Hello, sweetheart. How are you?" she asks.

"Good. I wanted to let you know Erin and I will be leaving soon."

"You have everything you need?" Laurence asks. He's bouncing Valentine up and down. It's the first time I've seen her since getting back. She smiles at me and holds out her arms. Panic swells in my chest.

"She wants her big sister, Amelia," Mother whispers. Swallowing, I pick Valentine up. She immediately squashes my face with her little fists and plants a sloppy kiss on my mouth. The whole family titters as I grimace. A line of spit connects our lips.

"Thanks, V." She giggles as I wipe my face, trying not to gag. She's adorable, but kind of gross.

"Sit and have some food," Mother instructs. She's still in helicopter mode. "I made cinnamon rolls."

"Morning," Erin calls from the doorway. She smiles at me and makes her way over. Valentine abandons ship as soon as Erin is within reaching distance. I know who she favors, and I can't blame her. I want to be in Erin's arms too.

"Did you get it?" she asks me. I nod. "Good. Let's eat and then get going."

Twenty-Eight

ERIN

We're all business now. The sex reinvigorated us and brought us closer. We needed it, but now we need to get moving. We've got a life to get back to.

I'm not going to question Amelia's sudden mood change, which has done a complete 180 since yesterday. Okay, maybe a few questions have crossed my mind since she did a strip show for me last night. For example, is it possible she's burying her feelings? Yes. That would be my first guess. When I got back, she was wrecked, but now she seems to be functioning as normal. Is that a red flag? Definitely. Under normal circumstances, my first instinct would be to sit her down and talk it out, even if she hated it.

Amelia is known to get lost in her head and hide her feelings until they burst out in a whirlwind of chaos.

However, these aren't normal times and I have to trust her. We haven't got the luxury of taking it slow and going on a deep dive of her psyche. No more than we already have, anyway. So, I'm going to go along for the ride, and hope we can piece our lives and ourselves back together again after we save our species.

"We'll take the bike," Amelia says as she gathers our things into two duffle bags. I'm not sure why she's bothering. The clothes haven't magically changed to anything useful. It's still just a pile of vacation gear. Although leaving our sex toys doesn't seem like a good idea. Not with Lucille lurking around. She'd waste no time doing something with them to rile Amelia up. Yes, we should take our things. "I want to stop at Insomnia first."

"Whoa, hang on for a minute. That's ridiculous. Not only is it fair to assume the building is being watched, but it's in the completely opposite direction of Washington, DC"

"It's also where our clothes are. I'm sick of looking at bikinis and linen. We need proper attire. And like I said, I'm tired of running. We can get inside and up to the penthouse without being seen. See it as a test run for the big white building surrounded by many, many guards we have to get past."

Okay, maybe I *should* be worried about her. This is reckless.

"I'm not being reckless. Insomnia is our home. I will not be run out of my home for a moment longer."

"Amelia..."

"Erin, please trust me. We'll go to the apartment, get a change of clothes that aren't polyester and from the set of a low-budget action-adventure movie, and then leave."

A smile graces my lips. "You're not a fan of the combat pants?"

"No. I am not. They're itchy."

A snort escapes my lips. "You are ridiculous at times. And a clothes snob."

"Call me what you will. Just say we can go to Insomnia first." I can't resist her puppy dog eyes.

It's such a bad idea, but I trust her, and she needs me to show her that. "Fine. We'll call it a dry run."

Amelia pulls me in by the waist and kisses me until I'm breathless. "Good. Now let's go."

Unlike the last time we left the bunker, I'm not on the verge of a panic attack or tears. There also isn't an audience bowing and praying for us, which I'm wholly grateful for.

We said quick farewells to the family after breakfast. None of us wanted to draw it out. This isn't goodbye.

The smell of fresh air is possibly the sweetest thing—apart from Amelia—to envelop my senses. We have several miles to walk before reaching the bikes hidden in the trees. They're the same ones she, Chris, and Simon took to LA to find Jordan and Mack. I listen as she recounts the journey. It doesn't get deep. Amelia talks about the sights, and the feeling of being on the open road again. Honestly, it's a pleasant change to have such a light conversation. The levity has been missing between us for far too long.

Amelia skips the last few feet to the hidden motorcycles. I enjoy seeing her excited again. I also like how I'll get to wrap myself around her for a few hours. The bike is nice, not as sleek as *her* Ducati. She straps our duffles to the back and then swings her leg over to straddle the seat. God, I've missed watching her do that. It takes me right back to the first time I saw her on a motorcycle. She was trying to seduce me, and it worked. Mack, my then-date, didn't appreciate it at the time, but we can all laugh about it now.

"Hop on, beautiful."

Her voice is like velvet. Oh, I'd like to hop on something!

I get situated behind her. My thighs squeeze her tightly, as do my arms. We forgo helmets for now. Both of us want the wind in our faces and the sun on our skin.

"No speeding," I say before she revs the engine. She turns her face to me with a wicked grin, slips down her aviators, and guns it, causing me to shriek.

Asshole!

Her shoulders shake with laughter as she slows the bike to a safe speed. We might be invincible, but neither of us wants a face full of asphalt.

US 93 isn't the most picturesque of highways. It's just one long road of desert and a few hills. The towns we pass through are tiny, with no more than a convenience store and a gas station. We only stop once to gas up. There are no other customers and no surveillance equipment. So far, so good. We've hardly come across another soul the entire ride.

Amelia climbs back on after filling the tank. "We turn off soon. When we hit I-15, it's a straight shot to the city."

"We should put helmets on, baby. There will be cops patrolling. No need to draw attention to ourselves and get pulled over."

I hand her a helmet, but before she slips it on, I give her a kiss. Whether it's the stress finally creeping in, I don't know, but I need to feel her lips on me as often as possible. Our physicality calms me.

The advantages of entering the city are the crowds and traffic. We're agile on a bike and I'm confident Amelia could outrun any vehicle if needed. Hopefully, that won't be necessary. I'm thinking this as Amelia effortlessly guides us through the streets. I feel a wave of confidence come over her. She's comfortable here. This is her domain.

"We'll walk from here," she says after pulling over. We're in a private parking lot. It's the perfect place to stash the bike. No one will question the high-end motorcycle. It blends in with the luxury cars lined up like expensive dominoes.

The sun is setting, but the city is only just getting started. It's Friday, and the bars are filling with the weekend crowd. I know we look out of place in our outfits, so I'm eager to reach Insomnia. Amelia was right. We need to ditch the combats.

Amelia is on high alert. We stop and start several times as she sniffs and tilts her head to listen. I use my abilities to reach out and search for other energy sources. Another little trick taught to me by Balam. Together, we conclude that Insomnia is empty. There are no obvious surveillance spots surrounding the building, either. It's quite heartbreaking seeing our once thriving empire standing vacant and dark.

"Let's high-tail it through the employee entrance. Even if there is someone watching, it's doubtful they'll see us if we're at full speed."

"Baby, I can't run as fast as you."

"Hold my hand. I'll get us there," she says with a wink. "Ready?" I nod. "On the count of three." When we hit three, I launch myself as fast as possible. Amelia is in front, but I keep up. We're inside the club in seconds. The door barely shows any signs of being touched. "See, easy." She laughs.

The familiar smell of alcohol and sweat permeates the air. It's been weeks since the club was open. The bar area is a mess. Bottles lay smashed on the floor. We tread carefully through the carnage. The place has been ransacked.

The panel that hides the access to our apartment is open and we both know what we're about to find. Like the bar, it's a disaster zone. We thought they'd search the place but, this? They've ripped into the couch. Smashed mirrors and torn up books. I feel a growl building in my throat. *Motherfuckers!*

"Hey, Erin. Honey, it's just stuff."

"No, Amelia. It's our life they've come in and destroyed."

She pulls me into her chest. "No baby. Our life is the two of us and our family. This is all just material things that can and will be replaced."

I suck in some air and pull away. "You're right. Let's go change and get out of here." I can't stand to look at our beautiful home in such disarray.

The contents of our closets are splayed over the floor of our bedroom, but the majority of items are unharmed. We work quickly to pick out some fresh clothes and change. It feels so good to be in my own things again. The duffel bags get unceremoniously dumped on the floor. I'd love to fill the bath and spend a few hours soaking, but then again, it doesn't feel so friendly in here anymore.

Amelia has chosen black jeans, boots, and a band tee I bought her last year. She whips her hair into a high ponytail and shrugs on her worn leather jacket. She grins at me when she catches me staring. "Come on, honey, we've got places to be."

"Uh, huh." My response earns a laugh and a smack on the ass.

"I'll meet you downstairs."

Good call on her part. I need a minute to get myself under control. I've opted for dark wash jeans, chucks, and my favorite green tee. It's a comfortable outfit that smells of home and reminds me of lazy weekends. I throw on a jacket and take a second to look around one last time. The mess is fixable. We'll get it back to normal in no time. That's what I keep telling myself, anyway. How I get the thought of men invading our sanctuary out of my head is another matter. One for later.

Amelia comes out of her office as I reach the bar. "They got nothing important. They completely missed the floor safe."

We've never kept anything at the club vampire related, so the most they would have taken are bank statements and vendor forms. Walking over to the bar, I take two shot glasses that are miraculously not broken. I upend a bottle of Jack until they are both full. Sliding one over to Amelia, I pick the other up, cheers, and slam it back.

Licking my lips, I pat the bar top. "Time to go, baby. We've got a long way to travel."

Amelia swallows her shot. She stuffs some bills into her inside pocket and casts her eyes around the room before turning away.

We head toward the back of the club. "We'll take the bike as far as Arizona. Chris made a few calls before we left. He's got a buddy who owes him a favor."

"Plane?"

"Yes. But don't worry, I have no intentions of flying it. We'll have a pilot that isn't insane. It's also bigger than a toy and comes with a bedroom."

"Oh thank god." I laugh. "Lucille has scarred me."

"She's scarred many people, my love. I should have warned you all!"

We exit the club and make our way back toward the bike. We're both quiet, and I wonder if the weight of what we're about to attempt is finally hitting us. Getting to the capital is easy. The rest? Not so much. And even if we do manage to get to her. The woman is going to assume we're there to cause her harm. She'll have Secret Service on to us in no time. And then what?

The plan isn't feeling so thought out anymore.

Amelia snorts. "Honey, we didn't think it out at all. Let's be honest, we're following Lucille's moronic idea to waltz up there and break in."

We look at each other and then burst out laughing. Oh, my god she's right. We're nuts! This is the most idiotic idea ever.

Twenty-Nine

AMELIA

A wave of nostalgia hits me as I sink into the plush seats of the private jet. I think of the family vacation we took to Ireland. How Aliah deafened us all with her warbling. The bickering that almost sent Mother crazy. How Erin got to see the Loch family in their natural state. No heirs or graces. Just a family of squabbling kids and their exasperated parents. How we made love in the bedroom. How scared I was of losing Erin. I can't believe how different our lives are now. If I'd have known what was to come back then, I might just have scooped Erin up and run away. But then I think of Chris and Jordan. Of what their lives would have been if we hadn't met them.

I find it so hard to balance the scales. My heart feels heavy with all the shit that's come along with our new life. Noah, Dr. Mendhi, the soldier, and the fucking president. It's been nonstop. But then I think of the vampires who are living a life free of torment because of what Erin and I did for them. I think of the families they will have. Is that enough to balance out the bad? I don't know.

My mind wanders back to our trip to Ireland. To meeting Barty and Anya. To the amount of whiskey we drank.

"That's a pleasant smile. What are you thinking about?"

I turn my head to Erin and smile. It's not lost on me that she is allowing me time to tell her my thoughts instead of reading them directly. She's in the chair next to me by the window. Her hair is hanging over her shoulders in soft waves. She's a picture of pure beauty. "I was thinking about our trip to Ireland with the family."

Erin snorts a laugh and then covers her mouth, looking embarrassed. She's fucking adorable.

"I thought Victoria was going to have an aneurysm. You Lochs are an unruly bunch!"

Chuckling, I lace my fingers with hers. "We are. Do you regret marrying into it?"

Tapping her index finger to her chin, she makes a show of thinking about it. Only when I've gasped in faux indignation and tickled her does she laugh. "Of course not. I love you all. Always have, always will."

We sit laughing together. Erin reminds me of how Mother threatened to turn the jet around if Lucille didn't stop hitting her brother. It's my turn to snort. We discuss other trips we've taken with the clan and conclude they are always a chaotic mess. We also decide that when we go on vacation next, they will not be joining us.

The flight attendant interrupts our jaunt down memory lane. "Would you like some champagne?"

It's strange not having my crew with us. I internally roll my eyes at how that sounds. One percent problems, am I right?

"No, thank you. Some coffee would be great." I plan to drown myself in champagne if we pull this off. I still can't believe we listened to Lucille. *Get out of this godforsaken bunker and do it!* Those were her words, and that's what we did, with only the barest of plans. Break into the White House. That's it.

"Still think we're crazy?" Erin asks with a smile.

"Completely," I answer, chuckling. "Certifiable really. We're bar owners, not Navy SEALs. And yet here we are on the way to the capital to scale the walls of the most protected house in the country."

Erin cocks her eyebrow. "Scale the walls, really?"

"Okay, not that dramatic. We can probably jump up to a window or something."

Erin gazes out over the world, passing us by. "What do you think she will say?"

"I don't know."

She turns her head and laughs. "Oh Amelia, you are a terrible liar. Sometimes I don't need access to your mind to know what you're thinking, baby. You believe it's a waste of time and she won't give us a chance to explain anything, right?"

I shrug my shoulders. The flight attendant passing out coffee gives me a few seconds to gather my thoughts. "Thank you," I say. She gives me a smile and then leaves. Taking several sips, I enjoy the rush of caffeine before Erin clears her throat, growing impatient with my stalling. "I think she flew off the handle as soon as Mohan opened his mouth. I think she dispatched elite soldiers to find us and do god knows what. She doesn't seem like a rational woman, Erin. It's likely she will scream bloody murder the second she lays eyes on us, and we'll have to fight our way out of there."

Her hand moves to mine. "Is that what you're worried about? Having to fight humans and losing control?"

"Of course!" I state. I may have put a lot of what happened lately to the back of my mind, but this brings it to the forefront pretty quickly. What happens if we have to fight our way out? In my heart, I know I won't let the anger overwhelm me. Not when I understand it a little better now, and I will have Erin by my side. But what if they hurt her? That's a surefire way for me to lose it.

Erin strokes my hand. "We need to be smart about our approach. Use our abilities to get us inside and talk to her calmly. We've not really touched on using our gifts since I shared Balam and Itzel's memories. How do you feel about using them?"

How do I feel about using my gifts? First, I'm struggling to see them as anything but a burden. Second, I feel disconnected again from the warrior inside. I can't claim her as my warrior anymore. She feels like a stranger again. Something that is dangerous and unpredictable. I thought I'd mastered my "gifts," but now I know it's not true. This energy inside can overtake and overwhelm with devastating consequences. Why would I ever want to tap into that again?

But if we don't use what has been imposed on us, the outcome could be a lot worse for Erin and me. Breaking into the White House alone is enough to get us thrown in prison. Let alone the fact the president believes us to be two supernatural monsters. If we can't shield ourselves, we're sitting ducks.

"Honestly. It's the last thing I want to do. I know we have more to learn, and I'm open to that, but right now. I want nothing to do with this thing inside me."

"That thing is still a part—"

"Please don't finish that sentence, my love. I can't stand the thought of it being in me, let alone a part of me. I understand I will need to protect us when we get there. But that's all I can commit to right now, Erin."

I may understand our abilities better, but I'm nowhere near ready to accept them as a part of me. Biology and evolution be damned.

She leans over and kisses me. "That's all you need to do. Throw a shield around us, and I'll take care of the rest."

"How?" I'm not the only one who has an unpredictable gift. Erin might not feel the anger I do, but that doesn't mean her abilities aren't equally dangerous. Entering minds and memories is a power I don't think anyone should possess. Not after witnessing the carnage and pain it can cause.

"I'll make us invisible to anyone we come across inside."

"Erin—"

"Honey. I will simply mask our energy. I do *not* intend to manipulate anyone's mind. I promise."

"Do you understand why our abilities are something we need to consider letting go of?" I ask. "We're here promising each other we're not planning on doing something terrible. But neither of us can truly keep our word. These gifts are dangerous."

"But they're also designed to help our people. Help the Fallen."

I nod. "Yes, but how much of that have we been doing lately, Erin? It seems to me we are using our abilities for that purpose less and less."

The rest of the plane ride was tense. Our conversation got heated, and I had to walk away for a little while. Erin wants to hold on, but I'm not sure I can. I understood in the beginning when it was about helping vampires and their mates. But it feels like we've strayed far from that path. I think that's the true warning of Balam and Itzel's memories.

It's like the more we discover, the farther away from the original goal we get. They became obsessed with their abilities. Balam focused on conquering minds rather than helping her fellow vampire. Itzel destroyed entire villages in her pursuit of 'protecting' her mate, when in reality she became addicted to the power of her rage. Aren't we doing the same? Every time we discover a new facet of our abilities, we concentrate on it and master it. When does that stop? Shouldn't it be enough that we are saving families the heartache of destroying their Fallen loved ones? Isn't that enough purpose for us?

As the plane glides toward the runway, I know I need to get us back on the same page. We cannot go into this with tension between us.

"Erin?"

She looks at me, and I sigh with relief. Her eyes are soft, and I can see she's just as upset by our silence as I have been. "I'm sorry, my love. We said we'd talk about all that after we'd finished this. I shouldn't have pushed."

Taking her face in my palms, I brush our noses together. "We will decide together. But right now, we have to focus. I can't go breaking into the White House with this hanging over our heads."

Surprisingly, she laughs. "We keep on saying those few words like it's the most normal thing in the world." I look at her, confused. "Breaking into the White House."

I chuckle. "I never want to say White House ever again after tonight."

The captain announces over the speaker system that we have landed and will be ready to disembark soon. Shit, it's really happening. We're really doing this. We thank the crew and depart.

"Ready?"

Erin looks at me. "No, but what choice do we have?"

There is no choice. Tonight is the only night the president is alone. The First Lady will return in the morning and then she's flying off to the UK. It really is now or never. Our families and friends need a resolution as fast as we do. They deserve to go home free of fear. We all deserve to live our lives in peace. I just hope Erin can get through to the woman.

Standing outside the hangar, we take a few cleansing breaths. "Okay, let's go over it one more time."

Erin shakes out her limbs. "We make it fast," she begins. "I'll distort the energy around us. You will throw a shield over us. We do what we did at Insomnia."

"Correct. Full speed. We'll be a blur. I'll take care of any locked doors. You just concentrate on keeping us off anyone's radar, okay?"

"Okay. We can do this. Right?"

I take her in my arms and inhale her scent. I wish we'd taken the opportunity to make love on the plane. Not only does it replenish our strength, but it fortifies our bond. Maybe then Erin wouldn't look so nervous.

"We *will* do this. Together, like always."

The night is flitting away from us as we stand there holding each other, but I'm reluctant to let her go.

"Okay, I'm ready," she says.

Am I?

Thirty

ERIN

The president isn't what I thought she would be. Maybe I was expecting a tyrant, pacing the halls of her private accommodation as she barked orders into her phone. I've built her up so much in my mind, I'm kind of disappointed and relieved at the same time.

She's just a woman. Sitting in a t-shirt and men's boxers on her couch, watching a recorded football game. Of course, she still doesn't know she has company. We made light work of getting in. If after this meeting we've accomplished what we needed to, I might suggest a few areas the Secret Service could bulk up security.

It's good to take a little time to observe her. Find out what we have to deal with. The next part is where it could get dicey. I feel Amelia's eyes on me. She's letting me take the lead from now on. I feel her drop the shield that's protected us up until now. I have to stop distorting our energy to reveal us, but I'm finding it harder than I thought. My confidence in my plan suddenly feels lacking.

Amelia takes my hand. *You can do this.*

God, I hope so. A light breeze touches my skin and I know we're in full view now, but the president still hasn't noticed. She picks up her bottle of beer and takes a generous slug. Hopefully, she isn't inebriated. That will make everything ten times harder.

Okay, so I need to just get this over with. I gently clear my throat. Nothing. She's far too engrossed in the game. I roll my eyes because this is ridiculous.

"Ahem."

Wow, I've never seen a person jump so high in my life!

"What the?" Her eyes are the size of dinner plates as she looks frantically at me and Amelia. I see the second she decides to scream for help. So does Amelia, because she's cover's the distance in a flash, her hand covering the president's mouth.

"Please don't, ma'am," she says in her usual confident voice. "We're not here to hurt you, I promise."

"Madam President. We just want to talk."

Amelia pins her with a stare before slowly removing her hand. I can see the president warring with herself. Naturally, she wants to call for her agents, but another part of her is curious.

"How did you get in here?"

"Do you know who we are?" I ask in the least threatening voice I can muster. She looks between us some more and then scrambles back to the point she's perching precariously on the couch's armrest.

"I think she's figured it out, my love."

"You...you're them. The V-vampire Queens."

"Good grief," Amelia huffs.

"Ma'am, we are vampires, but not queens."

"Stay away from me," she stammers. Her panicked reaction has her falling off the couch and landing on her ass. This is going downhill fast.

"I know you're scared. We understand why you think you should be, but I promise you. We're not who you think. We are not a threat. There is so much for you to learn, Madam President."

Amelia takes a step toward her and holds out her hand. "Please, Madam President."

Everything hinges on her next move. I know I'm holding my breath. My lungs seem incapable of doing anything as we both watch and wait.

There is a reason Mohan felt he could take the existence of our kind to the president. I know he regrets it now—hell, we all do—but there must have been a reason he felt the woman would listen. Is there still a glimmer of that hope?

I'm almost at the point of passing out from lack of oxygen when she finally makes a move. With a visibly shaking hand, she accepts Amelia's help to get up off the ground.

I don't want her to overthink, so I jump straight in. "We're not the monsters you believe us to be, ma'am."

Amelia comes to my side. "We understand the myths and legends you've no doubt drawn conclusions from, but I promise you. They're false."

"I was a human not so long ago." I'm trying to relate to her or get her to relate to me. Whatever works.

She frowns. "She changed you?"

"No ma'am. Vampires do *not* have the ability to change humans. Just another myth."

I'll leave out Amelia's unique ability to do just that for now.

"Mohan," she begins, but Amelia cuts her off.

"Came in here and delivered some news that was bound to shock and scare anyone. In his defense, he was just excited, but he should have known better."

"H-he started talking about queens, and things called the Fallen."

The president's body language is still tight, but she's not displaying signs of outright fear or aggression.

"We can explain everything, ma'am. But first and foremost, you have to believe me when I say we are no threat to you, this country, or humankind. We never have been. I implore you to call off the soldiers who have been hunting us."

"You killed one of them," she hisses. "You *are* dangerous."

Amelia holds up her hands. "Please. It wasn't as black and white as that."

I can feel the anger beginning to build in her. She's frustrated that she's having to play nice instead of ripping into her about her part in the soldier's death.

"Madam President. Amelia defended herself. If you want to be frank about it, this would never have happened if you'd shown some restraint. Ma'am."

Amelia might need to hold back, but I don't. I'm happy to placate her to a degree, but she has to take responsibility for the chaos she's caused.

"Restraint? How much restraint would you have shown Ms..."

"Loch. Erin Loch, and this is my wife, Amelia. I'd have thought you would've at least memorized our names before sending your attack dogs after us."

"Erin," Amelia says softly. "Reign the sass in, honey."

Right. Yes, good idea.

"I apologize. It's been a stressful few weeks, as you can imagine."

"What my wife is saying is that your decision has had grave consequences. I take responsibility for my part, Madam President. The last few weeks have been hell. I imagine it hasn't been much fun for you either, learning of our kind, without having all the facts."

She scrapes her hands through her salt and pepper hair. "I feel like I'm going crazy. What sane person thinks they are talking to vampires, for Christ's sake?"

Amelia nods. "Understandable. But you are not crazy. Just uninformed."

"I can show you the truth, ma'am. If you'll let me. But please call off the soldiers. Our families deserve to go home."

"So, I should just trust you?" Her attitude sounds harsh, but I can feel her faltering. Amelia drops her head to her chest. She's getting impatient with the back and forth.

"Call your agents," I say, earning a glare from Amelia. "Have them here, in the room, so you feel protected if that's what you need. But let me show you our truth, ma'am. If after that you still believe we are your enemy, I'll go willingly to whatever black site you want."

Amelia's hands ball into fists as she continues to bore a hole in the side of my head. She isn't appreciating my spontaneous outburst.

What the hell are you doing?

I don't know what I'm doing. Winging it, I guess. But she has to feel in control if we want to get this done.

The president regards me for a second before lifting a discarded button-up shirt off the back of the couch and putting it on. After covering her t-shirt clad chest, she presses a telecom button on the side table. "Horton, would you come in here, please?"

The door opens, and the agent immediately reaches for his gun the second he spots us.

"Stand down, Horton. These are my guests." Horton doesn't look convinced, which is fair. It's nearly 1 a.m. We are definitely not scheduled visitors. "How will you show me?"

I watch Horton circle the room. He is within reaching distance of the president. I'm guessing he wants to throw himself in front of his boss and start shooting, but for now, he remains in place.

"I want to share memories. Our history with humans." Horton looks utterly lost as he looks at us all. "I won't touch you. But I will share your mind, briefly."

"You'll... How?"

Yes, the president is very curious now.

"Amelia and I differ from others of our kind. I assure you I will explain everything. Will you consent?" This has to be her decision. If I force her, she'll think we're there to manipulate instead of sharing the truth.

"Horton, you have my permission to open fire if you feel I am being harmed."

I nod my head. "That's fair. Please take a seat, ma'am."

"Madam President," Horton begins, but is silenced.

"This is the only chance I will give you, Mrs. Loch. It's true, I didn't handle the news well. I've known Mohan for a long time. I thought he was a good man."

"He is a good man," Amelia interjects.

"I think that will depend on what I am about to learn. I won't risk the safety of my people on a few well-meaning words."

I sit at the opposite end of the couch. "Please remember, Madam President, we are your people, too. I voted for you."

"Me too," Amelia adds.

I don't think she expected that. Instead of replying, she leans back and waits.

"I need you to open your mind. I will warn you that the memories come with their attached emotions. So please, Horton, don't shoot me the second the president whimpers or laughs."

I catch the president's lip curl in amusement. I think we're making progress.

When Balam shared her life with me, it wasn't just her time as a queen. It was her and Itzel's life after they gave up their abilities. They traveled the world for centuries. They witnessed the trials and tribulations of society as both vampire and humankind grew and changed. This is what I will share with the president.

I flood her mind with thousands of years of history. She witnesses the atrocious acts against vampires committed by humans. I show her the truth behind the Fallen. Of how we are born, how we love. Our customs and community. But above all else, I highlight the cohesive way our species lives and thrives side by side. I show her how vampires have helped develop technology and vaccines. She sees that some of the biggest breakthroughs in history are the work of vampires, and most importantly, how vampires have held no desire to be better than humans. I show her that in all our combined history, vampires have lived in harmony with their human counterparts.

I feel her wonder as I take her through each memory. She feels what I feel. This is why Balam made sure I would take the memories on as if they were my own. She has to feel more than she sees. Emotion is a powerful weapon. Amelia wanted us to fight the vampire way. The smart way. I can't think of a better offense than to tell the truth. The good, the painful, and the joyous.

My brain is fried by the time I pull out and return us to the present. Amelia is by my side in an instant, propping me up. Horton rushes to the president, who leans forward, her elbows on her knees, cradling her head.

"Are you okay, my love?" Amelia whispers in my ear.

"Yes. I can't do anymore, Amelia." I lean into her, soaking up every bit of love she's sending my way. The only noise in the room is the president's and my heavy breathing.

"Madam President? Ma'am, are you okay?" Horton is getting agitated that his Commander-in-Chief still hasn't spoken. He's going to do something rash. I can feel it. "Hands up," he suddenly barks. Amelia sighs next to me. "I said, hands up."

"Horton," the president rasps. "Put that down. It wouldn't do anything, anyway." Horton hesitates. "Now, Agent."

"Can I move without getting a hole put in me?" Amelia asks. "Again."

I elbow her, because this is not the time for pettiness. We need to know if we're walking out of this room as free citizens of the United States.

"You can leave now, Horton."

We all watch him leave. His heart rate is through the roof, and I know he's not happy about the president's command. Not one bit.

"Are you alright, ma'am?" I ask the moment the door shuts.

"I'm not sure, Erin. And please call me Candice." First name basis, that's got to be a positive sign. "How am I supposed to process all of that?"

"Take your time. You can ask us anything."

She shakes her head. "I need a drink. But I doubt it will help."

Amelia stands, resting her hand on my shoulder. "May I ask what you plan to do next, ma'am?"

She looks up. Emotions are still running rampant through her mind. "Nothing. I'll do nothing."

Amelia looks pissed off, and I know she thinks the president still intends to smoke us out and harm us, but I can feel her heart. She is a good woman. And now she knows the truth. We have nothing to fear.

"It's okay, Amelia," I say.

"I apologize, Amelia. I didn't mean that to come across as it did. When I say I'll do nothing, I mean I have no intention of pursuing you or your kind any farther. But if I may offer some advice. Revealing yourself to the world would be a mistake. Unless Erin can do *that* on a global scale, you will always face an adverse reaction. It's in our nature. I've seen it," she says, looking at me. She has seen it. She's felt humanity's aversion to things they don't understand and what they'll do to make themselves feel safe, even when there is no threat.

"I doubt there will be another vampire alive who will want to come out," Amelia says with a chuckle. "And honestly, there isn't anything to gain by doing so. Our world is a volatile place already. We need to work together to fix it, and revealing ourselves would do the opposite. No one wants that."

The president gives a small nod of agreement. "I will make sure there is no evidence of this or anything that has happened recently. We start with a clean slate. If you agree."

I stand with the help of my wife. My energy reserves are toast. With a shaky hand, I clasp the president's waiting palm and shake it. Amelia mirrors me. "Good luck with the re-election, ma'am," she says.

"Thank you. And good luck to you," Candice replies, holding my stare. She knows Amelia and I have a big decision to make. I let her see our vulnerabilities and fear regarding our abilities. It softened her to us. "Also, please allow me to offer a safe escort to the airport, or place of your choosing."

We accept the offer. No need to be worrying about tripping the alarm on the way out.

Our love story has been far from straightforward. Amelia has risked her immortality. We have waited with bated breath for our chance at eternity, and now we have fought. Fought for our people and our freedom. Whatever decision we make, I will always put Amelia first. She is the reason I breathe. She is my Queen, with or without abilities.

Epilogue

AMELIA

"**B**abe, I have sweat dripping down my ass crack."

I hate the jungle. It's hot, humid, and full of things that bite. The only thing I want biting me is my wife.

"Amelia, we have one day left. Please stop complaining. Balam and Itzel have been nothing but gracious hosts, and all you've done is bitch."

"We were supposed to visit for a few days. It's been two weeks. I know you want me to make my mind up, but this is only pissing me off."

Things are a little tense between me and Erin at the moment. After we smoothed things over with the president and got our lives back to something resembling normal,

Erin began hounding me about our abilities. I know we said we'd decide one way or the other, but it felt so good to live like regular people for a little while.

Erin, of course, is as stubborn as a mule and insisted our vacation be a few days with Balam and Itzel. She thought that by learning more about them, and in turn, ourselves, and these gifts, she could encourage me to discuss my desires. I know she wants to keep her gifts, and I understand her reasons.

Fallen vampires and their human mates still needed our help. But I'm not sure that's enough of a reason. Not when our abilities come with such high risks to our own health. Erin might perceive it as selfish, and it probably is, but my commitment is to her, not to the Fallen. I know the difference now. Before I believed it was my purpose to be the protector. It isn't. It's my choice. One I'm not ready to make.

I was wary of Balam and Itzel to begin with. I saw them at their worst, and I admit it colored my opinion of them. When we turned up, I was surprised to see two old women. Erin explained that Balam and Itzel had chosen to end their immortality a few decades ago. Even so, the aging process was still much longer than a human. It saddens me now to know they will eventually die.

We've been going on guided meditations with the old queens for days. I'll admit I've learned a lot. I feel confident that I could remain myself while helping human mates turn. It's that tiny part of me that still holds on to the fear of losing control. Of Erin losing control.

But my indecision and worries are only pissing her off. It doesn't help that I am tired and irritable after sleeping on the floor for weeks. We haven't had sex since being here either, and that is definitely bad for my mood.

Erin turns and places her hands on my sweaty face. "I know you're unhappy. But you promised we would make this decision, Amelia. We can't move on with our lives with this hanging over us. I can feel the Fallen calling to me. If I'm not going to help them, I need their voices out of my head. We need to give up these abilities so I can have a night's sleep without feeling guilty that I'm leaving them in torment. I need you to decide."

Okay, I feel like an asshole now.

"Why didn't you tell me this is how you're feeling? All we've been doing is going over and over the reasons we should or shouldn't choose this life."

"Because I didn't want you to think I was emotionally manipulating you." She sighs. "Their pleas are becoming too hard to ignore, Amelia. I need to know one way or another."

We left Riley with plenty of venom, but that doesn't stop Erin from feeling the Fallen. Even from the other side of the world.

Balam and Itzel emerge from the trees carrying fruit. They've given us space to talk every day, but until now, we've always come to an impasse. Mainly because I shut the conversation down. I can't do that anymore. Not when Erin is suffering for it.

"Will you join us?" I ask. Balam and Itzel sit without question. Erin looks at me with hope in her eyes. "I think it's clear what you want, Erin. And I understand you are the better of us. Your reasons for keeping these gifts is to help our people. And even though I feel like we lost ourselves in other aspects of our abilities for a while, I know your heart, and I know you only want the best. So, I agree we should choose to be the vampires our people need."

"Amelia—"

I place my finger on her lips. "But I have conditions. One: Balam and Itzel will remain our guides, our conscience for as long as they walk this earth. We will check-in with them every month. They will help us stay grounded and call us on it if we aren't. Two: If we stray again from the purpose of what these gifts are intended for, we give them up. No questions asked. I'm not prepared to lose either of us to temptation. And third: We update how we help the Fallen. There is no need to be biting anyone." Ugh, the thought of another drop of human blood touching my lips makes me want to gag. "Dr. Chord will continue to milk us and *she* will be the one to help the Fallen and their mates on our behalf. I'm not being coldhearted, but I am looking out for us. We deserve a life, Erin. We've waited long enough." I take a deep breath. "There. That's my decision."

"This is why you deserve to hold such power," Balam begins. "Because you don't really want it, but you'll do what's right for your people. I would be honored to remain as your guide."

"As would I," Itzel states. "And your friends."

"Erin?" She's silent, which I think should worry me.

"Thank you," she says, but it's more of a sob. "And I agree with all your terms."

I clap. "Excellent. Can we go home now? No offense, ladies, but I'm really done with the jungle."

"You sound like Lucille," Erin murmurs.

"You'll be punished for that," I reply. The spark in my wife's eyes tells me she's looking forward to it. And maybe my two-week dry spell is coming to an end.

Marcus and Laurence are embarrassing themselves on the dance floor, as usual. Lucille is grinding up against Trent, and I'm dying for a drink. The party started hours ago and ended up relocating to Insomnia. Even my parents are here somewhere.

The queue at the bar is three deep, even with five bartenders working at full speed. Being the owner has its advantages, like slipping behind the bar to serve myself. I'm just bending down to one of the under-counter fridges when I feel a presence behind me.

"What the hell do you think you're doing?"

I stand up straight and turn around. "I'm getting a drink," I reply calmly.

"I can see that. Surely you aren't stupid enough to think you can just nip back here and help yourself. What kind of bars do you usually go to?"

"I rarely go to bars," I answer.

"Maybe that explains this then," Erin says, waving her hand between me and the fridge. I take a moment to look at her fully. She's dressed in the bar's signature black shirt and trousers. Her hair is tied into a high ponytail. The golden hues shine under the many strobe lights. Her eyes are piercing blue. And, without sounding too lecherous, her tits are amazing. Even hidden underneath the shirt, I can tell she has a pair of tantalizing assets.

"I'm not sure why you're getting so upset," I say casually. Cracking open the water bottle and taking a sip. Fire burns in her eyes.

She steps forward and grabs my chin. "I can hear your dirty thoughts, Mrs. Loch. Is that really what you were thinking the first time we met?"

I can't help the wolfish grin. "Well, considering we were reenacting our first meeting, I thought I'd give it my all."

We're celebrating our anniversary. Not our wedding day, but the day we met. AKA, my birthday. The day I smelled cherries and laid my eyes on the most exquisite creature to grace this earth.

"You'd better give it your all. In the office, now."

With mock outrage, I clasp my chest. "We didn't do *that* on the night we met!"

She raises her eyebrow. "You did *Dana* on the day we met."

I wave my hand like I'm batting away the last ten seconds of conversation. "Forget that. I'm doing *you* tonight."

"Such a charmer," Lucille cackles. She's leaning over the bar, reaching for a bottle of vodka. "I still don't know how you got the girl, dear sister."

"I'm fantastic in bed," I say.

Lucille laughs louder. "Well, you are a Loch. It's in the genes. Enjoy ladies. I'll see you at the house for breakfast."

I laugh at Lucille's antics. The laughter dies in my mouth when I turn back to Erin and see the look on her face as she traces her eyes up my body. I'm wearing the same black body suit as when we met. Placing the bottle of water down, I tug her until our bodies are touching. I can feel her heart racing and I can smell her desire.

Bending until my lips reach her ear, I snake out my tongue and trace her pulse point. "Fuck the office. I want you in our bed."

She wraps her hands around the back of my neck and pulls me down into a scorching kiss. She nips my lip and sucks on my tongue. As usual, I forget about the world when Erin is close. It's not the first time our patrons have seen us get hot and heavy in the club, and it won't be the last. Anyway, it's my birthday.

Grabbing her ass, I lift her until she wraps her legs around me. Our lips haven't left one another and they won't until I get her upstairs and throw her on the bed.

I vaguely hear catcalls from my siblings. The crowd parts with wolf whistles and laughter. None of it registers though, because Erin is moving her hips, and I am dripping for her. As soon as the hidden door to our penthouse shuts, I use my full speed to get us to our bedroom. She squeals as I launch her to the mattress. My body suit comes off in record time, and Erin's t-shirt and pants take even less time to find themselves across the room.

"I knew your tits would be amazing," I say with a wink. Lowering my body on top, I revel in the feel of her skin. Our rhythm is second nature now, and it doesn't take long until we are both panting.

Since deciding to keep our abilities, life has been different. It's been calm. We've kept our word and retained our life while helping as many Fallen vampires as possible. We work at Insomnia and go on vacation. The tradition of having family meals with the rest of the Loch clan and Erin's parents is still alive and wholly chaotic. Barty and Anya moved here permanently. Chris and Simon are getting married. Not to each other. They mated with a set of twins, which I still think is weird.

Jordan and Mack are traveling the world. It took them a while to move past their experience with the soldiers, but they conquered their demons. They helped me too. I learned to live with what I'd done without letting it consume me.

Balam and Itzel are dear friends who have helped us navigate our way to a life that is quite regular. Just what we always wanted. They refuse to leave the jungle, which still baffles me, but it's their life. One that is still full of love.

Mohan was re-elected by an overwhelming majority. As for the council, all I know is there was a radical change. My parents are still involved, but I stay well clear. It took a while, but eventually, the community stopped referring to Erin and me as queens. Although there are several "fans" who insist on calling her by that moniker. Some even come to the club, solely to get close. Apart from that, we slipped seamlessly back into society and back to running our clubs and bars. Mohan still tries to pull us back in now and then, but I make it clear my interests reside elsewhere. Like right now, on my wife undulating below me.

When I think back to my twenty-ninth birthday, I remember how utterly hopeless it all felt. But then my irritating sister dragged me to the club, and I met Erin. On that day, my life began. My soul found its mate, and I found my forever. We've been through hell to get here, but I'd do it all over again in a heartbeat.

"Show me the stars, baby." Erin moans.

I'll show this woman the stars and beyond. And I'll do it for all of time.

For infinity.

Afterword

Thank you for reading Fighting for Infinity.
Please spare a few more minutes of your time by heading
over to Amazon and Goodreads to leave a review.

Acknowledgements

A huge thank you to my team. A special shout out to Lori
and Carol for their eagle eyes.

Other Titles By Alyson Root

A Dance Towards Forever

Diving Into Her

Always Emilie

Broken Parts Included

Love & Other Wild Things

Finding Molly Parsons

Keeping Carmen Ruiz

The Wisdom of Bug

Sleigh Bells Ring

Risking Immortality

Waiting for Eternity

Fighting for Infinity

About the author

Alyson was born and raised in the heart of England. She moved to Paris in 2015 when she met her wife. Together they moved to the west of France, where they now live with their two dogs. Alyson spends her time reading sapphic fiction books, writing and Scuba Diving.

Alyson discovered her love of writing in her mid-thirties. Her debut book, *A Dance Towards Forever,* was inspired by her wife and their very own love story. Alyson wrote *Diving Into Her* and award-winning *Always Emilie,* which added with her first book, created The French Connection series.

www.alysonroot.com

a.rootauthor@alysonroot.com

HUMAN
AUTHORED™

THE Authors Guild®

2673928